I0728824

Deja vu On Cherry Street

No part of this publication may be reproduced, distributed, or transmitted in any form or by any means, including photocopying, recording, or other electronic or mechanical methods, without the prior written permission of the publisher, except in the case of brief quotations embodied in critical reviews and certain other noncommercial uses permitted by copyright law.

The story, all names, characters, and incidents portrayed in this production are fictitious. No identification with actual persons (living or deceased), places, buildings, and products is intended or should be inferred.

Originally published on November 18th, 2022

Deja vu On Cherry Street

The Mardi Town Series

Zineb Bizriken

*To the baristas who fuelled my coffee needs while I wrote this novel.
To many more books and coffees.*

Sol's Point of view

We wandered around, the sleeves of his black hoodie covering his hands and mine. On this serene night, the cool sand underneath our feet glistened as it reflected the moonlight. I heard the crashing waves so distinctly. Our stroll was peaceful. I always dreamed of taking a night walk on the shore with the person I loved. With a tap on the shoulder, I turned to face that charming face of his. Without telling a word, he points toward the starry sky. My eyes naturally followed, only to see the most breathtaking image ever to exist. In the middle of stars and a full moon was a rainbow. It rested on a puffy cloud, proudly displaying its seven colours. While I was awestruck by the sight, he asked me:

"Have you ever seen a rainbow?" It was his oh-so-familiar voice I loved. It exuded an aura of dark honey with woody notes.

His rather simple question required me to rack the back of my brain, as I didn't recall ever encountering one.

"I might have when I was younger. There's no way to look back."

Although the rainbow was fascinating, something else had caught my attention: him. I peered, trying to get a good look, but...

My eyes had opened, and I woke up. His rosy lips were the only thing I remembered from this occasion. The lower one was a tad bit fuller. Darkness made it hard to see. Every day, I could identify a new feature as if it was a puzzle. I often dreamed of this mysterious person. Never did he tell me his name or who he was. He had just tagged along every so often. It wasn't troubling, nor did I mind him. The unknown to me was a mix of an eerie atmosphere and fluttering butterflies.

The time on my phone had erased all the fictitious thoughts and brought me back to my reality, which was college. I was lucky enough to wake up later than most students, whether it's college or high school. I attended an online college that enabled me to work at anytime and anywhere. No scheduled classes, all there is to it was to listen to lectures, complete assignments, occasional quizzes and big exams meant to be completed in specific centers. Though I could grab my laptop, study in bed without having to get up and dress, I preferred to go outside. I still lived with my parents as I saw it as a waste of money to live elsewhere when the tuition fees are high enough already. My parents were never home because of their work and so, the house always appeared hollow and the silence was too loud. Every morning, I walked along Cherry street to make my way to the Cherry street coffee shop whose name wasn't very original. In Mardi Town, almost every street had a café. I chose this one due to it being the nearest to my house. Quiet times were the absolute worst for me. I always had earphones in my pockets when roaming around. These days, I listened to R&B.

***

In no time, I faced the coffee shop, which could also be called my second home. I spent more time here than in my actual home. I enjoyed the ambiance, the warmth, and the sound of people. When I opened the door, the small silver bell attached to the top of it had rang. I was home. The camel brown walls welcomed me back. The fragrance of freshly brewed coffee drove me crazy. Going to the counter, I waited to order my go-to coffee, a cold brew. I wouldn't live in a world without it. "Sol!" the barista, who seemed to never have a day off, called out. Bruno was always present, every single day. Either he was a hard-working person or has connections with the owner. The employees changed as often as you would change coffee filters. A new face every day except for this one who beamingly smiled at me.

"Hello, Bruno."

I pretended to read the menu on the wall I knew by heart.

"Isn't it lovely outside?" he started. "I walked out of the house with a good feeling. I wasn't wrong about that. You're here!" Bruno was a nice person. His negative trait was that he rambled on things that mattered little. All I wanted was a cup of coffee.

He tugged on his Hawaiian shirt, still rambling. Today, it was an ocean blue one with pink plumerias. I'd be curious to see his wardrobe. It's likely a line of Hawaiian shirts in various colours and motifs.

"So, what should I get for you?" Finally, but really? My order remained unchanged. I've never asked for a frappuccino instead, it was always,

"A black cold brew, please." My passive-aggressive tone was barely noticeable. He talked so much before asking for my order that he almost ruined the day.

"A black cold brew it is!" he said, every part of his face lighting up and the ash brown hair on his head jumping a little. I showed him half a smile and took a seat near the broadest window of the shop. The location was perfection. You could daydream while watching the sky and the passing cars. While I waited for my coffee, I observed my surroundings. I guess it's a pass-time or simple curiosity. My track of time gets easily lost while watching the various license plates. Many have words written on them. Ironically, the most common is: Cafe. Then there are repetitive numbers such as 111, 444, 555, 777, etc... After a quick search online, I learned they are called angel numbers. I took notice of them when they came to me daily in various formats, such as the time written on the clock, the final amount of a bill or, as mentioned, license plate numbers. I heard each sequence had a different message. It was all too confusing to me. To see them so often made them meaningless and so I tried to ignore them. The words that snapped me out of my deep thoughts were:

"A cold brew for Sol!" I leaped out of my chair. Just a taste of my favourite coffee brought me back to life. Caffeine had no noticeable effect on me. I was immune. It contributed to my levels of dopamine. In simpler words, it was my feel-good drink. The flavour brought me joy.

I had to log in to the portal of my college's website after taking out my laptop. I never was ready for it. College and the social science I studied were both to my dislike. People often chose this program for the sake of going to college, not because they had a career in mind. Bearing no dream or passion of my own, I searched for a goal or a vision towards life. At the moment, my feet followed a trail of rocks traced by lost souls with nowhere to go. My lack of interest in studying permitted me to get distracted and glance away from the screen. Procrastinating wound up being the easiest activity in the world. It wasn't shocking for it to be my only talent. Any five-year-old would have more talent than me at this point.

My observant mind looked around, found people, created thoughts about them because I wasn't over-thinking enough. People-watching is my hobby if it legally can be called a hobby. On the assumption that it is not, let's say my eyes stop on strangers for a while because they are in my range of view and I zoom out because of my lack of sleep. On this Monday morning, salary men drank their doppio espressos while skimming through today's newspaper before heading to work. Two retired old men talked loudly about their adventures last weekend and their plans for the next. A guy wearing a black hoodie that hid his face bopped his head to the music from his earphones, eyes glued to his laptop. That hoodie reminded me of the fake guy I foolishly fell in love with. Was I so lonely that my subconscious created a person for me to love? At last, there was a college student cramming for her exam with noticeable dark circles and a falling messy bun. This would be my future self if I didn't get to the studying part of college. My gaze had returned to the screen, which had turned dark because of inactivity. Brushing the touch pad, it lighted up again. Piling assignments and unseen lectures flooded the page and my vision for a fact. With a deep breath, a sip of coffee, and the bone-cracking of my hands, I eventually started. Hands were on the keyboard, studying playlist in my ears and the robot-like trait in me, switched on. I continued wasting time and using time wisely on and off for a couple of hours before calling it a day.

***

I was home by five and would have to wait around an hour before my parents came back to populate the house once more. My dinner was made of previously frozen items. In more details: mashed potatoes, something resembling a steak with the texture of cardboard and a cranberry sauce on top. After three minutes and a half in the microwave, it wasn't so bad. Cooking takes too much effort, and as they say, simple is best. Some do also say a healthy body is a healthy mind and I've shown you my lack of both. Still, satisfaction wasn't my lack. One may presume I lived in the good old days. I went through days with no considerable problems.

Eugene's point of view

I forced my eyes open, only for them to shut by reflex. The closed blinds had deluded me into thinking the night hadn't ended. My phone said otherwise. Mornings were the worst.

With a groan, I lifted my body, only to plop it down again. The need to wake up at a reasonable time wasn't mine, it was my mom's. She called every single morning, making sure her son lived like a human being. I named my alarm after her 'five minutes before mom calls'. These measly minutes were enough to submerge myself in cold water, and repeat ah, ah, ah until my voice wasn't as hoarse anymore and I could pretend I'd been awake for a while now. Heavy steps lead me to the kitchen where I open the faucet, lower my head and let it rain on me. The larger sink made it easier to put your head underneath it. It seemed I had miscalculated that day since vibrations from my phone had already started. My mom called and my voice was non-existent. My mind alert, I let out vocalizations that sounded like a crow.

"Morning, mom," I said, answering the phone in speaker mode.

"Good morning, darling!" Her cheery voice emitted rising sun vibes. "How are you feeling today?"

I scratched the back of my head.

"I'm good." Simple is best.

"What are your plans today?" it's a script. She repeats the same lines every day as if she read it from her ' parents living away from kids' guidebook.

"Some freelance work, like every other day." I recited my lines from the back of the book.

"You're not just saying that to end the call; you do have work lined up for today, right?" She didn't have complete trust in the freelance industry and was always worried I'd abruptly stop getting opportunities and would be left to starve.

"I have work," I clarified. "When you are a freelancer, you have more opportunities for various works you wouldn't have been able to do if a title restricted you. How many times do I have to explain?"

"Alright, alright, there's no need for a speech. I've heard enough of them today."

"Today? It's only the morning. Did you fight with dad again?"

"It's nothing, only a difference of opinion."

"You sure?"

"Yes, I'm just annoyed by the long speeches you and your father give when explaining your argument. Can't you people fight like normal people?"

"My speech wasn't that long."

"I know, I'm sorry."

"There's no need to."

"I'll let you go now. Don't forget to throw out the garbage," as she said that, I looked to my right where indeed laid a full garbage bag I'd forgotten to get rid of and that was a mother's seventh sense. "Don't let the dishes pile in the sink, check the expiration date on the milk and…" She continued to sing the same old song, and I bopped to every lyric. It ended with: "I love you."

"I love you too."

The end.

The proper start of my day awaited me: coffee. I placed a capsule in the machine and let it drip into a cup that said, 'latte again'. Neither was I late all the time nor a latte drinker. I only liked coffee puns.

I turned on my laptop placed on the counter top. You could guess that the kitchen was my favourite space in the apartment. The counter stood as my office, and the sink, my bathroom.

A page I hadn't closed last night presented itself. As soon as possible, the edited picture needed to be sent out. I do photography and have been doing this work for a couple of years. I am only twenty-two, but I started in high school. When I realized that photography was my passion, most of my attention went towards it. It's not like it would go elsewhere, no way did it go to studying. For years before graduating, I cultivated this work of mine in order to go full time right as I entered society. My reality for the last month was being stuck at home everlastingly, editing. During the summer, many photo shoots had been done, the idle part of the job, the less fun part took over my days. I tapped my fingers on the edge of my laptop and stared at the screen, giving force to my eyes. No matter what thought crossed my mind, it was never the right one. Something was missing in this picture. Unable to figure out the key, I snapped the laptop closed. Turning on the speakers—who were always in the kitchen—I listened to music, loudly. People weren't home much at this time. I've never received noise complaints. Either they are nice people or the ghosts had no voice to complain. Inspiration comes to me in different ways. Music was one of them. I stood and danced. My feet moved on their own, my arms flew and my lips moved according to the lyrics. Would it be possible to call this dancing? It was more like a crazy person swaying or flapping around. I don't want to admit I was crazy. It's reassuring to think everyone has crazy quirks.

After insanity came inspiration. Not today. No. I sat back in despair, wondering if this cycle would ever end. It came to my attention that revelations or eureka moments had been rare nowadays. I had hit a wall. In a literal sense, my only view was plain white walls.

I had forgotten I even made a coffee and was too late. No steam came out of it. Re-heating a coffee in the microwave is a crime for coffee lovers, so I drank it cold. The colder it got, the more bitter it was. An idea struck me for once. It related to my work, indirectly. I left the cup on a surface and walked away. I packed my laptop, my multiple hard drives, earphones, not forgetting my wallet, along with a film camera. The deal was done. If these walls blocked the flow of my creativity, I would go past them. I couldn't destroy them or even paint them. I didn't have permission to.

I moved to Mardi town only a couple of months ago and had not discovered it much; it was a shame because it is such a festive-looking city. I could take many pictures here. At every turn, a photogenic setting found itself. I had a workload to finish before I could start doing what I loved. Pictures taken elsewhere to edit and send. Staying cooped up in my apartment was a choice, one I had to make for the sake of focusing on the tasks already on my plate. The promise broke and nothing could be done. I had locked my eyes on the

Cherry Street Coffee shop across my street. Whenever I passed by on the way to the convenience store, it intrigued me. It looked familiar.

When I entered the shop, I felt comfort. With the closing of the door, any hint of regret was gone. Although someone took the seat I'd been eying from the glass outside. A coat was on the chair and an opened laptop on the table. This must be a safe town for people to leave something as precious and expensive unattended. I settled for a table stuck to a wall which had an outlet. The warmth of the wall, the dimmed lights on the ceiling, the Bruno major songs on the speakers and the mumbling- like chit chats were perfection. I hadn't felt such an ambiance in a while. The only regret was not coming before. Never did I know the charm of coffee shops until that day. The desire to take out my film camera and take pictures was hard to resist. Clenching my fists, I held back. I captured the beautiful elements with a pair of eyes. Indoor plants on shelves, baskets filled with shredded papers of all colours; my eyes couldn't get enough, but they had to. Time had passed, and I had a cup of hot coffee with me along with an opened laptop, ready to get some work done. New pictures in my head became a bridge linking my problems to their solutions. With freshly found inspiration, my hands moved fast. The missing link was no longer missing.

Altering my photo, I found it funny of how my view of the café reflected onto it. Warmth was written all over it. Yellow and orange tones were used to add that vintage touch I was fond of. I experimented with the brightness, contrast, and saturation to arrive at this sweet spot. I was more than satisfied with the results. My head lost itself in this little world I created. Multi-tasking wasn't a forte of mine. I focused on one thing at a time. After having seen what I wanted to see, there was no need for a second glance. For hours and hours, my ears blocked the noise around me and my range of vision was shortened. To be honest, my black hoodie did obscure most of that view. A ruckus could happen and I wouldn't be aware of it until after it ended. For hours and hours, work had my full attention. My sense of time disappeared with the coffee I unconsciously drank. Looking at the empty cup, I wondered if someone stole some of it.

Giving my eyes a break, I turned my head away. A question mark and an exclamation mark popped into my head when I first laid eyes on the moss green-eyed girl sitting near the window. Seems like the coffee shop wasn't the only thing that felt familiar. Only one look and I could hear a bell ring. It didn't feel like I saw her somewhere much the same as maybe we went to the same kindergarten or she was a friend of my sister. A memory of hers was at the tip of my tongue, melting like a sugar cube.

Sol's point of view

Blinding darkness blocked the entirety of my senses. There was no sound, smell, or sight. I stood still, waiting for a light or a sign. Just then, a scent came through. The lemon fragrance made its way to my nose. My face softened, and I was relieved. The heart that beat irregularly because of fear regained its normal pace. I knew he was coming.

A long trailing black sleeve came towards me and I, without a doubt, tugged on it.

"Don't," he said, making me back-pedal.

His form gradually turned more visible, but ended in a blurry state. The person in front of me, I could recognize by only his voice or his scent.

"I want to hold your hand," he told me.

"Hold it, then."

"I shouldn't."

"Why not?"

I felt my lips melt into a frown.

"It's too much of a risk."

"I don't understand."

He spoke less after that. Without words, his sadness was detectable. His eyes welled with tears. Or was it mine?

After a long pause, his mouth opened once more. "I am poison to your life and you are mine."

Some words and a reality hurt like thorns on a rose. My feet moved on their own and I had the urge to run into his arms, only he faded. It was like he never was here. A hologram delivering a message.

"Don't leave me," were the last words he muttered before-

"Sol! Sol!" I woke up with quite the surprise. The unpredictable had occurred. Had I changed my alarm to the voice of my mother? For the first time in a hundred years, she called my name—first thing in the morning. It would only be possible on weekends. On a Thursday morning, she'd be at her workplace. My sleepy head had first thought it was the second part of my dream: the nightmare. I shut my eyes again. After a while, those same eyes opened and realized its body shivered. An important layer was removed from my bed, the blanket. It was a fuzzy red velvet layer that kept me warm throughout the night. Pulling it away so briskly was cruel. I crunched up in a ball—it's a human defence mechanism.

"Wake up!" she shouted. "We don't have time for this! We need to go, now!"

I rubbed my eyes and saw my mother standing in front of me. The once blurry image had proved itself to be true.

"What's happening?" I told her, bringing myself up.

"I'm telling you, there is no time. Just hurry!" In my crouching state, a million of theories crossed my mind. One of them being that my father was in the hospital because of an accident or a sudden illness. I always feared the worst.

"Wear something clean and come out. Your dad's waiting in the car," my mom said from afar. Although I could now drop my shoulders and breath knowing my dad was fine, anger couldn't be avoided. This situation had turned predictable. It would most definitely be work-related. My millions of theories flew away. I bit my lip and pulled my hair up, right and left like horns. A few grunts escaped my mouth. No, a great deal came out. My whole routine I had spent it rolling my eyes, contemplating life and shaking the anger away. They didn't care that I had a life of my own. Brushing my hair and pulling it in a ponytail, I looked for something to wear. When my mom said clean, she most probably meant presentable. Lucky for her, all I had were presentable clothes given to me by her. I wore a plum-coloured shirt that wasn't low-cut enough to be revealing along with sleeves reaching the wrists. For the pants, my favourite kind, some smooth business style black pants. Pardon my descriptions, my knowledge of fashion is awfully limited. These pants look like the one business women wear except for the fact they are much more comfortable.

In a rush, I move along to the car where my

parents waited. My mother repeatedly tapped her feet, but kept quiet. The guilt of this situation might have stolen her tongue. If she scolded me any more, she'd know she was in the wrong since they were the ones to bring me into their work without warning. Nobody had dared to say anything. My dad turned the keys and started the motor of the car. He drove away and my stomach rumbled. How ironic was it to never have been hungry in the morning until the chance to take a bite was taken away? As they say: You miss it when it's gone.

I put my head on the top cushion, hoping for more sleep before we arrived.

"You can't sleep," I heard from my mother that eyed me from the rear-view mirror. "Your face will appear bloated in the picture."

Picture? I almost rose from my seat. If I truly did, I would've hit the ceiling. Instead, I brought my body near the front seat; the belt holding me back.

"What picture?" I said, my eyes wider than ever. My parents both worked for the same marketing company and when you heard pictures coming from their mouths, straightaway you'd think of publicity. I did not want my face anywhere public.

My mom let out a cough before speaking, "Well, we have a new client, a very important one," I sluggishly nodded, waiting for her to get to the point. "His company offers a service that aids families to become happier." It became more and more suspicious. "And he specifically asked for the employees working on this project to use their family portraits for the online ads and commercials. Then I realized we had no family portraits at all. Thus, here we are." Yes, here we are. Our lack of family portraits was true. It was for the better. My parents were frequently too busy for such activities. I'd also hate for a family portrait to be hung in the living room behind the TV. How awkward would that be? In full honesty, taking a picture with my parents wasn't an issue. The online ads and commercials were. Since I knew practically no one, embarrassment wouldn't pose a problem. I had an exception in mind: Bruno. I could imagine him with a grin on his face. He would say something to the effect of:

"Hey, I saw you in an ad! Never would I have envisioned you doing modelling. Why didn't you tell me?"

Goosebumps rose across my skin. I wouldn't

pose for a camera. In order to win this case, it was necessary to find a wise way to show them my disapproval without sounding insolent. Respect is a concept well respected in our family. I thought of being formal and calling them mother, father, but it wouldn't change the tone of the words that would follow.

In the end, I went with: "You should've asked me. I don't want my face on there." My words too direct and did not seem thought of. Even if you take time to think, you end up in the same place as before. To beat around the bush wasn't an option. Time was ticking.

"We need this picture because we need this client. One picture won't hurt you," she replied, keeping watch on the passing clouds. In their perspective, the space for options was small. I was the unreasonable one now. They made me feel like a child throwing a tantrum over something that would cost me little compared to their loss. Their big-shot client being more important than my feelings was something I had to accept.

"We took time off from work. It's a big deal," my dad spoke for the first time today. That line made the guilt in me overflow. My finger nails digging in my palm, I admitted defeat. My whisper-like reply waved the white flag.

I laid back, trying to at least enjoy the peacefulness of a car ride. That tranquillity had given weights to my eyelids. As if it was her seventh sense, my mom caught me every time my eyes closed and told me off each time. She also told me to let my hair down for the picture. I abandoned the idea of catching some z's and followed the buildings passing beside me. Falling deeper and deeper into the view out the window, my mind escaped. It ran to him. I locked myself in my imagination. He flood my mind throughout most of the day. Oddly, these days, the feeling that I could meet him was reoccurring. Merely the thought of it made my heart shake. I imagined what would it be like if he were with me. Would I still be this lonely? Would I still feel out of place? Would holding his hand bring me the courage to face everything? A sheepish smile should've formed on my face. Instead, sadness showed. It was all just fantasies. It hurts a lot for fantasies. The only concrete element of it all was my agonizingly slowly crumbling heart. You might think I'm crazy and overreacting. He's just a guy from your dreams, you might say. Though I try to dissuade myself from believing it, I cannot deny this connection and this familiarity I sense. Sometimes, I envision myself gripping a severely damaged rope from the top of a building. If nobody brings me back on the surface, it will break, letting me fall down.

The sound of the gear being pulled back broke my chain of thoughts. We had arrived and my parents disgracefully ran to the photo studio. They must have genuinely wanted to clock in. They looked like kids racing to the house to use the bathroom first. Funny, isn't it?

Walking into the bright studio, my head turned. A lemon scent was on the horizon. In fact, it passed right by me. Before my head could fully turn, they shoved me on a wooden bench facing the camera placed on a tripod. I tried to look anyway. Sadly, that person was already gone with the closing of the door. The bittersweet scent lingered in my nose; not able to keep it off my mind, I zoned out.

"Miss? Eyes to the camera, please," the white-bearded photographer said, bringing me back to my senses.

It couldn't have been him. Lemon might be a common perfume. I avoided the glares shooting at me from each parent and looked ahead. A laugh nearly came out seeing the walls of the studio I hadn't remarked. A wallpaper resembling tiles you could find in bathroom walls covered them. My parents did rush to use the toilet. I showed a genuine smile to the camera, suppressing laughter. Their satisfaction with the photo was over the moon. They'll never know the true meaning of that beaming smile.

Soon after, they rushed to the car, making them look like kids racing to get shotgun on the front seat. I laughed from a distance before entering the car. My parents, I love them. They seemed to care more about work, but I knew it was for our wellbeing. I acknowledged the fact that it is hard being a parent. In this day and age, living just gets more expensive and challenging.

I asked my parents to drop me off at the café, since I already had my laptop in hand.

The day started on a strange turn but ended up being fine. I thought of that start as a minor interruption. And now, back to normality. Getting out of the car, I watched it drive away. Turning to the coffee shop, a sight made me halt.

Eugene's point of view

After a quick errand, I came to the Cherry street coffee shop. My productivity levels were much higher there. A part of me also wanted to see that girl again. Curiosity got the best of me. Entering, I saw that the seat next to the window was free. No belongings were left on the table. Mixed feelings were on my mind. Having come later than yesterday, it was a surprise to see it empty. It might have been her last time coming. Maybe she was passing through town. Maybe I missed my chance to discover the strange nostalgia.

Brushing away doubts, I took the seat. The concept of first come, first served, still applied. Placing my bag on the table, I went to order. The same guy who greeted me yesterday took my order. I learned of his name, Bruno, through the tag on his apron. Whenever he looked at me, his expression was dark. I compared it with the looks he gave to other customers, and it was downright different. What could I have done to him? I hardly knew the guy.

"What can I get for you?" he forced out of his mouth.

"A lemon and ginger kombucha," I couldn't bring myself to add a 'please' or 'thanks' to that.

He tapped on buttons of the cash register without mercy and, if I might say, aimlessly. Despite it, you could assume he knew what he was doing. I mean, he pressed on them without even looking. Instead, he glared at me. Oh, how I wanted to ask him what kind of bone did he have to pick with me? But I didn't. Maybe he hates men because of an unpleasant experience. I left it at that and brought my butt back to the wooden chair.

The weather was as gloomy as my frame of mind. The sky was grey with no rain in sight from those colliding clouds. Maybe it was the weather who switched my mood, or was it the piling work and nearing deadlines? I lacked motivation, though I found specks of inspiration in this place. I even had a view from that perfect spot, though yesterday's was just as fine.

Hearing the cling of a glass hitting the counter, my head turned slightly and from the corner of my eye, I could see my lemon Kombucha. That Bruno didn't say it was ready. His hate would have hoped I'd pick it up by the time it had no gas left in it. Unfortunately for him, I have sensitive ears. Ignoring any glare that came my way, I picked up the glass. I was more of a coffee guy, but my heart occasionally looked for Kombucha. It was nice. Funny story, drinking so much coffee made me immune to its effect and didn't help anymore. I drank it only for its taste, but I still needed something to wake me up. An old friend of mine recommended I check out Kombucha. I picked up a can of lemon and ginger and it was disgusting. The taste gave me chills rising to my brain. That one night, I kept drinking it whenever I felt my eyes closing. It worked and with time; I started to like the strong taste that slapped me in the face. I liked that the effect came from the taste itself rather than a substance that took its sweet time to work until one day it becomes so used to that body that it makes a bed in it, sleeps and gives up on its duties. One sip and energy manifested itself in me. The silver bell had rang multiple times as people entered but only once was I physically called to look up. It was her. The girl I thought I'd never see again. She stared at me with those gleaming eyes of hers. Her expression differed quite a lot from mine. I was content with my drink and the sight of her. Somehow, I looked like a fool. She had fire written all over her face. The guilt sank in knowing that I had took her favourite seat. She quickly walked away, settling for another. Coincidently, it was mine yesterday. A hair tie in her mouth, she brought her black hair with waves competing with those of the ocean up to attach them into a ponytail. She turned to me again, but this time, I was the one to look away. I still couldn't figure out where I'd seen her. She was so foreign and familiar at the same time. It makes little sense; I know. My efforts to wipe it all away and keep working seemed futile. The moss-green-eyed girl was on my mind. The film camera on the table exchanged words with me. It told me to take a picture. That's just how it works in our relationship. The camera tells me what to do. But I knew the law and the need for permission. Hesitating, I placed an arm on the table to support me while I stood. It did not support me and my legs did not take a leap. The chance—that hadn't presented itself in the first place—flew away. Courage was something I lacked. It was one of many imperfections in me. As a photographer, I needed a spontaneous mind and the fearlessness to ask a stranger for permission to take a picture. I gave up on the idea without having attempted it. Throwing the towel was something I despised. I had no choice but to bow in front of the law and fundamental respect.

Later on, my hand squished my cheek as my head fell or more like collapsed on the table. My eyes grew heavier, gaining pounds and pounds before they eventually shut.

***

Stars were in my vision, a million of them. They were awfully close. It was like seeing the milky way from earth. It would be a shame to look down when I am presented with such a view, but I did. On the emerald grass, there were other feet like mine. I was not alone. All these people, I didn't know them, yet they smiled at me.

"Look at the sky!" They said. "They're shooting stars!" Hearing that, my head moved back to the main sight. Indeed, they were shooting stars, dashing across the night sky. People were overjoyed. I found it odd and ominous. I was overwhelmed, terrified and received the impression that only I felt that way. People looked at me with stars of their own.

"Take pictures of it with your camera!" they said. Running away was the only thing I wanted to do.

Right then, as if my wish had been granted, a hand grabbed mine. A fairy-like person was responsible for it. She glowed, but it wasn't blinding.

"Follow me and chant these special words," a voice pure but mature came out of the light. I nodded in compliance, awaiting the chant.

"Universe, guide us through this sea of stars."

"Universe, guide us through this sea of stars."

"Take us away and let us live slow."

"Take us away and let us live slow." I repeated everything, letting go of suspicion—having immense faith in her.

"The meaning is you."

"The meaning is you." A smile had formed on my face without consent. The last line tickled.

She squeezed my hand before walking away from all the people deep into the woods. There, a portal-like door appeared in front of us, just like the movies.

"Shall we go in?" she said.

"We shall," I replied, stepping into the unknown. Here again was a whole new world—similar-looking but still different.

This time, I was not walking, nor did I run. My body floated in the air. Looking down had been the same as looking up. Surrounded by millions of stars, I advanced. I flew with a better view of something that wasn't as scary anymore. And at my side, the fairy-like existence radiated, making it hard to look away or discern anything.

Sol's point of view

Never did I think such a thing would happen. I stood in the coffee shop in complete disbelief. I blamed my parents, who wasted my time and made me come late. The perfect seat across the window was taken by the guy whose face I could not even see since his hood covered it. My sensitive side kicked in. The side who only allows me to be comfortable in a specific spot after having come day after day. I began to think that I had to do it all over again because I found a competitor. I saw him eye that seat the day before. War was starting and my weapon was an alarm clock. I stared at the table with fiery eyes until I felt a pair of big eyes locked on me. Startled by the fact I'd been caught, I walked away. Due to how fast I pretended nothing happened, I picked a random table. It was stuck to a wall and the worst of all; it was near the counter where I'd have eye contacts with baristas every time I turned around. At least, the chair I landed in gave my back to the counter. If it had been on the other side, there would be no need to turn around for a staring contest with, say, for example, Bruno. A single glance away from my computer and it would have been enough. Discreetly, pretending to look through the window, I checked to see if hoodie boy still looked at me, thinking I was a creep or simply childish. Thankfully, he wasn't looking, but I was. My eyes lingered for much longer than intended. Curiosity and fascination kicked in after sensitivity. His surroundings were interesting. He had a film camera right next to his laptop. It looked pretty cute if you asked me. My knowledge of cameras was as limited as it was for fashion, or anything else. It shows how boring of a person I was. No passion and no interest. Also, I didn't mean to pry by looking at his screen. I couldn't anyway, it was too far and dark. It was a relief to know that people weren't able to see my screen from that distance. I imagined what this camera would be to him. Was it a hobby or his job? I wished I could go strike conversations with him for the fun of it. Talking to people who found the love of their life—work-wise—may aid me to find mine. I wanted to know what it felt like to be so passionate. I'm no fortune teller, but the way he stared at that camera showed nothing more than infatuation. What would I look at with those same eyes? Seeing him made me green-eyed and happy at the same time. I didn't know this person, but a part of me felt proud of him.

I looked at him again. This time, maybe I was gawking. Just as yesterday, he wore that black hoodie of his with grey sweat pants. Either he had a dozen of them or laundry was a holiday thing only. Mornings must be easy for him. He'd open his closet door and for the fun of it say at loud: "What should I wear today?" with fingers rubbing his chin and then laugh at himself while putting on the same old black hoodie. Perhaps he'd eye the other clothes that were amassing dust in a corner thinking of going for something new and, at the very last minute, he'd decided against it. My impression of him grew brighter by the minute, but that was once again merely something I imagined. It couldn't be true.

My eyes went lower. I watched his long fingers tap the edge of his laptop while he blankly stared at the screen. Writer's block at its best, it seemed. I caught my lips forming into a small smile for no apparent reason. Redirecting my range of view to my work, I attempted to forget about my sudden interest in camera boy. I changed his nickname. Hoodie boy was the one in my dreams. Before forgetting about him altogether, I turned for one last peek. To my astonishment, his head was turned my way. We met eyes for a brief second before he pivoted back in a flash. Did he know I peeped every single time? Could he see me in the corner of his eyes? Were we tied in the game of catching each other red-handed?

I didn't continue the game. I reached for my coffee, realizing a bit too late that my hand grabbed air. He distracted me so much; I forgot to order my cold brew. With a huff, I brought my foolish self to the counter where I met a barista, who was not Bruno. It was a lovely girl named Caroline. That new seat of mine gave me an ounce of luck. It's the least it could have done. My order went smoothly. I asked and received my cold brew without unnecessary chit-chat. I had no excuse left. School work waited long enough. On today's menu were two assignments, one due tonight and the other Monday, not forgetting the pending quiz that lived in that stupid homepage for days. How I hated this, making the effort to walk on a road that leads me nowhere. Still, I worked. I did my best to not disappoint the parents who counted on me. The small child in me counted on me as well. She wanted her dreams to become a reality. She wished to become a well thought of cool person by the time she'd grow up. Though I am in my early twenties, for that little kid, I'm already grown up and far from being "cool". I sighed and looked away from the depressing amount of work I hardly touched. The sky. I wanted to get lost in it again. Not much to see when you need to squint because it's so far. The sun hid behind the clouds and they stuck together, *clouding* the sky. The one who stole my place fell asleep, head on the table and a closed eye covered by strands of black hair peeking out of his hood. Now I knew that he'd taken it for the rest of the day. He'd wake up in half an hour or so and work for a couple of hours to make up for the lost time. There would be no chance I'd get even close to sit in that chair today.

Another side of me, the righteous one, tells me that this seat brought me something other than luck. Without distraction, I could concentrate. Camera boy was asleep and I couldn't see the sky or passing cars. I had to work. Looking anywhere else would end up bringing attention to myself and by attention, I mean Bruno, who would come here to talk about his past or present and or future. Once again, he's pretty nice but such a blabbermouth.

Typing away the report, I froze. The universe really didn't want me working. In the span of a single second, complete darkness engulfed the area. The dimmed lights on the ceiling were off and the ambient sound of the machines were brought to a halt. On my screen, seven words appeared: You are not connected to the internet. It was a blackout, my first. Surrounded by obscurity, chills rose from my arms to my shoulders. Although outside it wasn't pitch black, the gloominess of the day and the lack of sunlight made it so it would be pretty dark in here without lights. I scrunched my eyes and took a best shot at seeing in the shadows. People behind the counter were vaguely visible, only their silhouettes. Camera boy, well, the fact he camouflaged with the dark made me suspect he was still asleep, unaware of what happened. How confused would he be? He might think it is a dream or that his outing to the coffee shop itself had been a dream and this was home. Other tables were empty and I could only hear whispers coming from the employees scattering around.

"We are sorry for the inconvenience. One of our staff members is on his way to check the fuse box. Another staff will bring candles to the tables." Their eyes might have previously only focused on the machines and not on the shop itself. That would explain why they didn't realize I was the only one listening. The staff with the candle will catch on sooner or later.

I have to admit that fear was indeed present. My own hand blended in the obscurity. My body froze, thinking any movement would lead to a pitfall. I wished, if only for a moment, he was there to hold my hand and tell me: *It's alright, you're safe. I'm here.*

Chapter 6

"Sol," a voice so close to me caught me off guard. I held my chest, trying to regain composure following this shock. Of course, I recognized Bruno's voice. I didn't see him coming, nor could I see where he stood. His voice felt nearby. "I hope you're not scared," he continued, the sound of the chair screeching against the floor.

"I'm alright."

"Aren't girls usually afraid of the dark?" I bit my lip, trying to control the face he could not see, anyway.

"It has nothing to do with my gender," I answered, baffled by his belief.

"Maybe you're just special."

"I'm nothing but ordinary," this answer abnormally came out like a reflex. For once, he seemed stuck. He had hit a wall in the conversation. And I was the proud construction worker who placed that wall.

"Strange that blackout. I did not see it coming. I mean, look outside. There's no storm or anything." He stormed through the wall. The foundation of it wasn't sturdy enough.

I smiled without my eyes instead of giving a reply, but I guess he wouldn't see that either.

"Why so quiet, Sol?" His voice either was louder or nearer. The latter would be the right one, seeing that I could hear his breath. It made me sick that he took advantage of this situation.

"I have nothing to say," were the words that got out of my mouth. Everyone has a dark side, and I discovered his in real darkness.

"I'll do the talking if that's better for you." *Crickets.*

What would I say to that? Thank you very much my dear Bruno. I love listening to you talk. I can never get enough of it. In my book, he now deserved an award for most bothersome employee, not of the month but eternity. My mind went back and forth with the thoughts: I hope the candle arrives soon and I hope it never arrives. When it comes, it'll be a distraction, but I'll also have to look at Bruno and vice versa.

"Boy, the candles are taking long," he said, tapping his hands, presumably on his lap.

It pains me to think we had connected telepathically. On second thoughts, anybody would have said that. This talk of ours was filled with walls and nothing much to discuss. In those cases, you would pull from elsewhere. You'd think of something you both would have in mind.

"I've got the candle," and the not-so-telepathic moment continues with another barista. She carefully placed the pumpkin spice-scented candle on the surface of our table.

"Now I can finally see you!" he exclaimed, breaking into an enormous smile. Where did he find the energy to smile this way every single day? I am practically dead inside and would burn calories trying to smile. Awkward laughter filled the air when I tried to respond to that incomprehensible statement of his. I wished on a star again, hoping someone would shut him up and save me from my misery.

"Mind if I sit here? It would save candles," someone said. By someone, I meant camera boy and previously also called hoodie boy. He stood in front of the table with a chair in his hands. I took initiative before Bruno would.

"Of course."

The candle light reflected on his face as if he was an angel descending. Wasn't he a sort of guardian angel? My eyes didn't have to go on Bruno anymore. Bruno sat in front of me and Camera boy, across. Since he looked nowhere, I directed my vision to him. His face was a little bloated from the nap, yet it wasn't a terrible sight. On the contrary, it was quite the view. Black silky hair coming out of his hood, black and clear eyes that resembled fish eyes—in a good way—a slightly fuller lower lip, a button nose that's slightly hooked with perfect bumping and the piece of resistance, a mole under his lip, the lower one. Don't ask me why my description is so detailed. Anyhow, he sat there fiddling with the strings of his hoodie, appearing nervous. The dead silence had more presence than either of us. I could even properly hear the flame moving on the candle. Bruno, though he deeply wanted to stay with us and chat, had things to do. Thank the stars for that. The staff there were people who were mostly all new to the job. As the most experienced one, he needed to be there. It was his duty to guide and aid others in complicated situations such as broken machines, shortages of ingredients and perhaps also a blackout. It was his time to shine, behind the counter and far, far away from this table. Noticing that he relentlessly peered back and forth from the table to the counter, I stepped up.

"You should go back to work. I'll be fine. The electricity will come back in a jiff, that's what I feel."

I never used the word "jiff" before, but so be it. He gave me a sympathetic smile and stood on his two legs.

"Maybe you're right, but don't worry, I'll be back later if the electricity's not back on," he said before walking to the counter.

"Boy, he can't get a hint," camera boy spoke up. His remark made a snicker come out of me. "I'm sorry if I crossed a line," he said, his lips curving into a small smile.

"No, no, I'm happy someone got the hint." A few seconds passed before I realized what I'd say. "Not that the hint applies to you." He laughed heartily.

"I'm beginning to think you're the one who's slow," he teased, and I felt my face turning bright red. At least we laughed together rather than laughing at each other. That thought calmed my mind and enabled me to, like the olden times, reach out a hand.

"I'm Sol." I hoped this act would steer us towards a less embarrassing conversation.

"I'm Eugene," he revealed, bringing his long sleeve back so he could shake my hand. The moment we had this simple yet complicated greeting, something changed. The touch of his hand was warm, contrasting to my chilly hands. This hand, I've held it before. The hair-rising chills, I've felt them before. My hand fit perfectly in his like Cinderella placing her foot on the glass slipper. It began with a sudden jolt of electricity and ended in bliss. Holding his hand, even if it was a handshake, felt nice. Let's say I had an unsettling awareness of my heartbeat. Neither of us let go. We were in a complete daze. The electricity could have come back, a cable could have exploded—letting out a loud noise—and we'd still be holding hands. With comfort and jitters came fear. One I could not explain. One that came from somewhere in me I had yet to discover. There came a voice telling me I needed to let got. It controlled me to do as it said, and so I did. When I lost grip, I faced him and noticed his mouth slightly open, drooping a little. Me, I felt the longing for a hand I held not even a second ago. The warmth lingered for a while, disappearing in the form of small air particles. Then came the yearning for his hand to be in mine again. I broke our intense eye contact we shared by looking down. His stare hadn't ceased. His attention was all on me, question marks written on his face. When eyes are on me for longer than five seconds, I redden, break in sweat and my face turns as hot as the top of a car on a sunny day. Today, none of these things happened. My face remained tanned— to some degree. Skin remained dry and my temperature was ambiguous. My anxious self hid itself and it was unprecedented, not with someone I'd just met. I could almost say that I felt comfortable around him. No amount of synonyms for the word strange could describe how odd it all was. Feeling a little better, I turned back, only to find him staring.

"Is there something on my face?" was the best I could come up with.

"There's nothing. I'm sorry," he said, eyes turning away. My words did not reflect my intentions. I might have come off as rude, just now. Our eyes didn't match, and neither did we hold hands. Sudden sentiments of regrets came upon.

"How was it to wake up in the dark?" Perhaps we could start again on a new foot.

"It was bizarre, but I quickly caught on seeing the candle on your table."

"You came looking for comfort?" I asked teasingly.

"Maybe I did." There, our eyes locked once again, and I fell deeper into his black hole.

Lights over our heads turned back on.

"Alright!" One rejoiced in the back.

"Let's get to work," another had said.

"Why so early?" one complained. "Couldn't the electricity have come back on closing time?"

"Jordan, you have to think about the café!" This nagging voice belonged to Bruno. "If the blackout had lasted that long, all the ingredients in the fridge would have gone bad!" He had a point, but the complaint of the employee wouldn't have changed fate.

"That Bruno, he's really something."

"I suppose he is something, but I don't know what?" I exclaimed, bringing us both to burst into laughter. When Bruno noticed us, it made us explode even more. Bruno was useful in at least one aspect. He was able to break the ice between us.

"You know, he looks at me differently than most people here. Does he have something against men?" I looked at him as if he were crazy.

"I don't think so. He's a very cheery person, a bit too much, though."

"Him? A cheery person?" He brought his chin to his neck. "I only see negativity coming from him."

"That's strange. Do you know him from somewhere else?"

Perhaps Bruno and Eugene knew of each other, but one—most likely Eugene—forgot about it and that's what he's mad about. Of course, nothing in life is that simple.

"I first came here yesterday and I don't recall ever seeing him before."

"Did you move to Mardi Town in the last couple of days?"

"Two months ago, but I was busy with work and couldn't get out much."

"Oh, I was wondering about your work," I blurted out, not realizing how creepy it sounded. "I saw a camera next to your laptop and thought: Is there a possibility he does something related to photography?"

"You are right. I am a freelance photographer. Today and the past month I've been stuck editing, explaining why I never went out."

If the black out never happened, we most probably would never have had this conversation. A flame, perhaps of passion, flashed its way into my heart for the first time. I was interested in this man's passion.

"Tell me more, if you have the time." Eugene sat up straight.

"Sure, but what about you? I'd love to know myself."

"Oh, I am asking you because I don't have a chosen path."

"I better tell you all about what it's like working in a field you love then, to inspire you."

Yes, inspiration is what I needed. While he talked about how much he loved to capture life and this world with a single click, I could see a sparkle in his eyes. Time passed without our knowledge and I experienced an eye-opening conversation with someone who it felt right to be around. When Bruno talked, my mind identified it as rambling. Eugene's words were honey to my mind.

Eugene's point of view

Her face was on the ceiling. I fell asleep thinking of her. I woke up thinking of her. The first vision of the day was her green eyes staring at me. The moss-green-eyed girl had a name; one that rolls off the tongue so easily.

"Sol," I spoke out loud like a fool.

For an alien reason, thoughts of her flooded my mind. Yes, she was captivating, but that enough wouldn't do this to me. It's much deeper, such as something who had been dormant. Her hand. When I touched it, electricity went through me. It wasn't painful like I made it sound to be. This feeling could not be defined. I understood nothing about it. Logic had left me for a couple of days and brought its distant cousins called: hallucination and delusion. Her portrait still on my ceiling entranced my eyes for way too long. It looked like I slept with open eyes.

That image of hers faded with the ringing of my phone. It was my morning phone call with my mom. I didn't even have time to prepare. I went ahead with it, sticking to the script.

***

The side walk is crispy. With no context, my choice of words seems peculiar. It is crispy since I walk on fallen leaves. They're everywhere. It's harder to walk directly on the asphalt. Fall neared its end, leaving behind last gifts: yellow leaves, orange leaves and, in certain areas, red leaves. Those are my favourites. Autumn is a beautiful season and as a photographer, I failed to capture it. Lucky for me, I brought my camera bag on this outing. I wanted to show Sol the camera I most used. The film camera was mostly for personal works, some may even say a hobby. It wasn't too professional, or expensive, only enough to see the world through a viewfinder. I took out the object the size of my palm, placing my eye on the viewfinder and twisting the lens, adjusting it. This scenery of falling leaves was picture perfect. The only sound going into my ear was the click of the shutter and the crunch of the leaves I stepped on in the process. I hadn't taken pictures in a while. Taking these lifted my spirit and made me fall in love with photography all over again. The mundane part of the work always made me doubt about my love for it. If I only ever had to click this button, life would be perfect, but it can never be perfect. Life wasn't meant to be perfect, neither was the world.

Taking all the pictures I deemed necessary to recharge my passion battery, I was on my way once again to the coffee shop. Something else made me excited. You guessed it, Sol. Would she be there today? Would she speak to me or would we both sit at different tables as if nothing significant had happened last night? My questions were soon resolved when entering the shop. I spotted her at the window seat we both were dying to have. Sol, immersed by her screen, didn't look up to the chime of the bell. And I wasn't sure if I could come up to her table and talk. Would it annoy her? She came here to work, not to interact with others.

Like a good loser, I accepted my defeat for the window seat and, like a person following the norm, I sat at my own table—not awkwardly striking conversation. We happened to speak yesterday because of a blackout. Today, the café was running smoothly, and I had no excuse.

I ordered a warm coffee matching the sweater weather outside and enjoyed my pleasant morning.

"May I get your attention?" Bruno said out loud, across from me.

Pleasant morning, my ass.

I wanted to pretend to be listening to music so that I wouldn't have to turn, but my earphones weren't in my ears. They were on top of my laptop, laughing at me. Due to lack of choice, I did turn. A single glance and my eyes twitched; His Hawaiian vest was too flashy for me. I've never seen a neon green one before. Squinting, I tried to keep my attention on him.

When he saw all eyes were on him, he started his speech.

"I am sorry for the interruption. I wanted to announce that next week is the Cherry street coffee shop's 100th anniversary!" He clapped to encourage us to follow. Few did. Not me. The coffee hadn't kicked in yet. "To prepare for the celebrations, we will place old photographs of the first 10 to 20 years in business on the walls. Please do walk around and get a look when we finish setting everything up."

The announcement was finished and everybody returned to their coffees and chit-chats. I, for one, was determined to actually have a pleasant morning. Sipping on my coffee and listening to the smooth jazz coming from the speakers on the ceiling helped. I couldn't help peeking once more towards Sol. The sudden attraction was weird. How was it so hard to take my eyes off her? I wished she'd caught my eyes, waved me hello and offer a seat at her table, but alas, she didn't even notice me. I couldn't do much about that. When I first arrived, I could have just said hello. Now it was too late.

***

History hadn't interested me. I remember at school, history was my least favourite class. What is so important to it? Shouldn't we look ahead instead of always behind? Regardless of my opinion on it, I stood on my two legs to see the photographs. That part captivated my attention. The fine black and white pictures on the wall deserved a shot. They captured the essence of the old Cherry street coffee shop. The place today is a far cry from the one showed in the photos. People held glasses not of coffee but alcohol. They danced to the live music of a band. On closer look, the singer roughly bears a resembles to me. It wasn't very clear. Walking to the next set of photographs, I stumbled upon the biggest shock of my life. That singer is my doppelgänger! They showed only the band in this one and his face was as clear as crystal. Astonished, my jaw dropped—lower by the second. The strangest part was the mole. This guy had a mole under his lower lip. So did I! Can things like that happen? Taking a sideways step, I thought nothing could surprise me anymore. Not so fast there, Eugene. The next image showed another doppelgänger, not mine but Sol's. My jaw reached the floor and mopped it. That identical person sat at a corner table typing away on a typewriter. Twisting my neck, I looked for Sol in a hurry— not noticing she stood beside me. My state of shock must have disabled my reflexes. Hers along. I tapped her shoulder with no response.

"Sol?"

Calling her name hadn't worked either.

My last resort was to drag her by the arm —accidentally crinkling her berry red sleeve— to a table.

"Sol?" I called again.

"Did you see that?"

I'd finally gotten a sort of reaction.

"I'm as shocked as you are."

"Shocked is an understatement." She said, shifting her view to me.

I couldn't think of something else to say. Now, I was the one lacking a reaction. Eyes round and lost, she waved a hand at me.

"Earth to Eugene."

"Sorry, as you said, it's an understatement and too odd to be a coincidence."

"Yes, and I don't remember ever taking a picture here or having touched a typewriter in my lifetime."

I was stunned.

"How does your head even go that road? It's beyond any doubt. Do you think I sang here every night when I just moved to town recently?"

"Can't you take a joke?" she raised her shoulders.

"I thought this line continued the joke. No?"

"You need more practice. Your tone was too stiff, making you seem serious."

"Got it, I'll work on it. But in all seriousness-" We both resisted our urge to laugh. "I'm curious as to who these people are and why they look like that."

"Like us, you mean."

"Yes."

"Stay here, I'll go inquire. The only person who'd know something is Bruno. He's worked here forever, leading me to think his family owns the place."

I watched her skipping away to the counter. In contrast to her, I was rather patient. Things tend to sink in slowly in my head. I was more of a calm person who was never in a hurry—

except for the next couple of minutes.

"Did he spill the beans?" *What kind of calm and collected person says that?*

"Sort of."

I waited for her to take a seat and comfortably lay out the news.

"He said the place was a bar besides being a coffee shop in the 30s. The band in the picture played some jazz every night. And the only piece of extra information we can find is supposedly behind the pictures."

"You stay put this time while I go rip those from the wall."

Her brows drew together, thinking I was once again serious. I laughed it off and followed my task. The more I admired the photos, the more I was amazed. The uncanny resemblances would make anyone piss their pants. It's a wonder we didn't.

I didn't flip them right away—wanting to see the truth with the other concerned party, Sol.

"Good. You didn't actually rip them out."

"I would never," I said, placing them on her table. "Are you ready for the big reveal? I'll flip mine and you flip yours."

Sol gave me a nod before holding on to the

edge of a picture. Without the need for a count, we simultaneously reversed them. Mine said: "Lokki and the blue boys."

"The cherry tree holds the text," read Sol from hers.

"Mine is pretty self-explanatory, but yours, I don't get. "

"Nonsense, it's easy. Plus, mine is better," she replied, scrunching her nose.

"How so?"

"From the image, we could assume she is a writer. From the sentence, we could assume she's left a text behind. And where would that be?"

She crossed her arms and stared at me, expectant. It didn't take long for me to figure out what she meant.

"Under the cherry tree!"

"Yup. I told you mine's better. It leads us to our next point. Yours is a dead end."

"It only leads us to that point if we find the text under the cherry tree. And which cherry tree?"

Our silly little competition made little sense. I enjoyed it. We laughed, knowing every word coming out of our mouths was childish.

"I'll find the cherry tree!" she exclaimed,

determined to win.

"You do that," I replied soullessly.

"I'll take the Bruno chance."

"That could work."

My ears perked.

Together, we went to bother him one last time. He didn't seem to mind when it was her, but for me, he frowned. He passed his fingers through his hair, firmly. It was revolting that the sight of me was provoking him.

When Sol asked him so nicely if he knew anything about an old cherry tree, Bruno found himself in a bind. He had no choice but to cooperate. For her sake.

He opened the back door and reluctantly left us alone in the courtyard. There our magnificent tree stood. It was short but had a thick trunk. Branches arched, giving center stage to plump cherries hanging on stems. I questioned the cherry tree behind the coffee shop and its purpose. What I wondered mattered little at that time.

"Now that we're here, we dig."

"Digging as in putting our hands in dirt?" I gazed at her, thinking she was crazy and I'm sure she thought alike.

"If Mr Eugene wants to stand back, I don't

mind," she replied, sticking her hands in the soil near the roots of the tree.

"Of course I'll help," I said, copying her acts. "I don't know if we'll find something so old, so easily." This last part, I mumbled.

"You never know until you try."

Chapter 8

November 18th, 1932

I sat at the corner table trying to get scrumptious words on the empty page, the delightful piano notes ringing in my ears. My fingers were on fire, typing away on the surface of a wooden table. I wouldn't dare to waste the ink of my Remington No.5 Streamline Portable typewriter. I worked day and night to afford this baby. Some of my odd jobs were shoe shiner and paper boy. Though, just by looking at my long hair and feminine face, you could tell that I was a girl. Wearing a hat, wrapping my chest with bandages and wearing a jumpsuit with suspenders on top of a white blouse fooled them all. For them, I was typical Tom helping his family by earning some money here and there. Those days were over now that I laid hands on this precious typewriter. My writing era was only beginning.

Around me was the idle chattering of housewives complaining that their husbands were home much too often and, at the table next to them, businessmen complaining about how the economy was failing them. I came to the Cherry Street Coffee Bar for the purpose of finding ideas or topics to base my book on. The next best seller was waiting to be written on this exact machine underneath my hesitant fingers. I suppose the 30s are not a good time to eavesdrop for the reason that I am not writing a newspaper article about how this economic crisis is affecting the people. In the midst of it all, the ambiance wasn't all so bad. The jazz music, the glass clicking, the espresso machine and even the repetitive talks—at the very least, the voices were nice to listen to.

A pair of black dress shoes stopped in front of me while I was still in a daze, "Here is your cappuccino, Miss...?" the man said with expectant eyes, placing my order on the table, careful to not graze the typewriter.

"Oh, thank you. Uh... My name is Cosima," I replied, taking hold of the little cup placed on the unnecessary little plate. I knew it acted as a coaster, though I did recall this was a bar as much as it was a coffee shop and there would be dozens of real coasters in the cabinets somewhere. Please accept my apologies for this unnecessary tangent who is neither revolutionary nor in any way debatable. It is only a cup on a small plate.

"Well, Miss Cosima, I hope to see you here more often. My name is Kylo and I will be at your service this evening." I gave him a polite smile to ward him off. Were waiters ever this nice or was it solely for the reason it was my first time coming here? Anyhow, the Cappuccino had been the last piece of the puzzle. It would be impossible to not to be able to write at least a complete sentence in this ambiance and so my hands were on the keys. Taking a deep breath, I prepared my head for the writing fever I felt coming. I might have looked a bit insane staring deeply into an empty page with my still hands hovering over the machine. I was bringing myself to another world, one of my creations. The problem being that I hadn't made a creation made it all too difficult. Regardless, my eyes were closed and a door in me opened to let in all the marvellous ideas. They sent a telegram saying they would be tardy to the party.

The sound of a bell ringing near the door interrupted my trance. My mouth twitched for a second and my eyes opened, lightly hurt by how tightly I'd closed them whilst focusing.

 Why was it so hard to write a book when it was a dream of mine? I've handwritten countless stories for years as a simple enjoyment. Now that I had taken the decision to write for a living, none of these tales struck the impression of being good enough. Pressure took place in my head and made it near impossible for ideas to flow.

With a sigh, I take a hold of my cup to sip the so far still warm cappuccino to then turn dramatically in direction of the small stage in front. I had heard a voice. It wasn't the chatter of customers or the waiter asking me if I needed something else. No. It was a honeyed voice amplified by a microphone.

"Good evening, ladies and gentlemen, we are the blue boys," he said. His face was as dangerous as his tone. With a black leather jacket and over-sized dress pants, he stood there looking like the love of my life. It was not only my head that dramatically turned, but my insides as well. "My name is Lokki and along with my band, we will give you the loveliest of nights," he concluded before strapping the guitar—which had the same colour as the coffee in my cup—around his neck. That bell earlier must have been the angels announcing the arrival of my faith. With only a couple of words and a single glance, I was swooning. But it looked like I wasn't the only one having a moment. All the other girls were leaning closer and gawking at him. Soon enough, my eyes softened and were back on my paper. Seeing the amount of people holding the same gaze as me made it feel less special. I wasn't meant to fall in love with him. His face and voice were meant to captivate everyone. Focusing on my future career as a famous novelist seemed to be of higher priority than love, thus I typed: Once upon a time. We always start somewhere, I presume.

"It is a night under the moonlight," he began to sing and I suppose I listened—Having nothing else to write.

"I look at you from afar, from my point of view,
My lady, you drive me crazy,
How did I ever spend my days alone?
Without your company, I was lost, yearning for more."

With every syllable coming out of his lips, my heart jumped. They were small jumps such as leaps. This time my head turned slowly and what a surprise, his eyes were on mine. His lips curved into a small smile as he continued to chant this honey-like soft melody.

"I know what I've seen,
You are the most beautiful tonight, my dear,
You are the only one for me,
Would you be my forever?"

Was this some kind of fan service? Was I the lucky winner today of the blue boys' fan lottery? These thoughts flowed through my mind while I kept getting lost in his clear Bambi eyes. Something else flowed, words for my novel. There was something about his voice, the sound of trumpets, saxophone, piano, guitar strings, and romantic lyrics. It finally hit me.

"Will you become my lover?" he sang—hitting a high note—and *eureka*! The inspiration that wandered in hollow roads made its way to me.

Romance in the air tickled my fingers, pushing them to the correspondent keys. The blue boys and this mystery man became my muses. Gladly, my ear took in the delightful words and got to work.

Once upon a time at the coffee shop, there was a moss green-eyed girl listening to the man who sang love songs.

Chapter 9

A new day had come, well, a new night. Whatever happens during daylight isn't quite relevant to this story. I had informed myself about the blue boys. The singer's name was Lokki, and I discovered that they played quite often at this particular coffee shop bar, bordering on every day. Thus, to write this perfect book, I had to dip into my savings and spend most of my nights drinking cappuccinos, observing a stranger and listening to good music. Sitting on that same corner table, I crossed my legs and shook the foot on top, my cadmium green low heel slipping off every stir.

"Have you heard of…" the women next to me were starting their gossiping session. As I was a writer, I thought it wouldn't be such a bad idea to put an ear out. "I heard Mr. Tums has found himself a mistress," the lady in pink began.

"I've heard that too," replied the lady in green.

"I even know who it is," said the lady in blue in her turn, captivating the attention of all her friends. "It's Caroline Dufort," she announced, making them all gasp with their white-gloved hands covering their mouths.

"I knew it!" started the lady in pink. "I felt a certain aura from her the day I had made acquaintance with her."

"Oh really? Well, now that you said it, she spent an awful amount of time in the bathroom dolling herself up," added the lady in green.

"I suppose she had many to impress…"

I stopped listening after a while. It was no use giving the audience to worthless words.

"Hello again, Miss Cosima," said Kylo, the waiter I'd seen yesterday. My was he out of style—not that I knew anything about style. I at least knew that there was usually a dress code for people working in such an establishment. Perhaps it was a family-owned business, and he was the family part of it. My eyes went to the brown pants shabbily tucked into bright yellow rain boots. The piece of resistance was the red and black striped shirt. He brought away the couple of ash brown, almost blond strands of hair falling on his blue eyes and opened his mouth: "What can I get for you?"

"Oh, just a simple cappuccino, yet again."

"Coming right up. I am glad you have come once more. I do hope you give me the pleasure of welcoming you here again tomorrow and perhaps the days that follow," he said, his speech trailing off as he left to the counter. Would he treat the rainbow ladies this way, or did I have a fatal charm that was unknown to most people, myself included?

I wondered why the band hadn't arrived yet. Was I too early or were they not coming today? With my luck, it wouldn't have been surprising. I was known to occasionally bring misfortune to some. I had tough luck and could share it just by breathing near someone. It wasn't a scientific phenomenon or one officially proved. It was merely accumulated experiences. Nevertheless, I gave a quick glance at the Victorian-style clock and saw that it was already 10 o'clock. They had come at roughly 10 o'clock the day before, and I hoped they were the punctual type. Right as the needle struck ten, the door opened, making me twist for a good look. The band stepped into the place in slow motion, every step having more impact than the caffeine I had been ingesting all night. And here I was scanning the way he moved and gestured, only to write it out later on. His dress shoes, heavy, loudly stomped to the podium. When Lokki placed his hands on the mic and intertwined his fingers, it all began, the start of my downfall.

"You make me dizzy, aren't you the start of my misery," he sang—struck by the midnight blue lights across the stage. His controlled voice full of soul made me breathe a little deeper.

"I dream of you and I don't know who you are," he sang the next night with red lights crossing across him. "Oh girl, I want to chase beautiful dreams with you..."

"If I let go, will you fly away, little butterfly..."

Every night a new song.

There was so much material to work with. All of his songs seemed to lead to one thing: a girl —the one he loved. All he sang were love songs connected to each other by red threads. He had often mentioned dreams and yearning, creating the impression it was destiny. I sat in my little corner and wrote not my story but theirs. I had an inkling of a crush on Lokki, but I knew I didn't stand a chance. The love he has for this person is deep. As a writer and a human being, I can feel the emotions in every sound coming out of him.
Putting my sadness away, I continuously made an appearance. cappuccinos after cappuccinos, I wrote gradually emptying the ink of my typewriter.

***

 Another grand entrance had been made. With his band mates behind him, he waltzed into the Cherry Street Coffee Bar looking polished from head to toe. Wavy black hair unusually reaching his nape—most men kept their hair short and clean—his leather jacket tagged along, as if it was stuck to his body. I had never seen him without it. On this Friday night, he went to the back of the café rather than to the stage. I wondered if there was an issue? I myself, had an issue. My cup was empty and my energy storage was as well. The caffeine boost didn't last long enough. Cappuccinos were lighter since they were added milk to. And they were small, portion-wise. Perhaps I needed something stronger that could be put in a larger cup and didn't require a plate underneath it. By pure luck, Kylo walked nearby, matching my eyes.

"I am always at your service," he said with a smile that oddly looked cute and puppy-like, his eyes wide.

"I do need something," I told him. Hearing that, he came to me, perked ears and a wagging tail.

"Anything!" Kylo responded.

"What would you recommend if I said I wanted something where the caffeine was stronger in a bigger cup?"

"I would recommend you black coffee. When you truly start to enjoy the taste of coffee, you'll realize that nothing compares to its raw taste, with no ingredient such as cream or sugar hindering it," he said, whispering the last words. I pursed my lips, hesitating a bit. Plain black coffee might be too bitter. He looked at me, expectant, with hands properly crossed on his stomach.

"Alright, one cup of black coffee, please."

"Coming right up and I forgot to mention, but with black coffee, you can get free refills."

A smile grew on my face, and my wallet rejoiced.

I was thinking that giving up on the guy I had a short-lived moment with might have opened another door for my heart. It's strange how suddenly, this person who merely filled my cup every day struck me as somewhat attractive. I contemplated the whereabouts of my heart. Was I falling in love too easily, or was this the rebound everyone talked about? Love was never my forte, and I knew practically nothing about it. I was learning it through Lokki's songs. Without them, I wouldn't have been able to start my romance novel. Previously, I took in consideration crafting a mystery novel. It wouldn't have much love in it, only a crime, plenty of suspects and a peculiar detective. Though it looked fun, this wasn't my forte either.

"Here's your black coffee," Kylo said, breaking my trail of thoughts. "I brought you a packet of sugar in case of it being too bitter for you," he added, thoughtfully placing the paper sugar packet next to the mug.

"Thank you, Kylo, I appreciate it," it was the first time I had muttered his name, and it showed on his face that he was taken aback—in a good way—his lips curved up rather than down.

"You're welcome, Cosi," he said back with a smile resembling a smirk, making me gasp internally. He had shortened my name and pronounced it so casually. This brief scene of ours somehow gave me butterflies. The coffee that was too bitter for me was almost sweet when recalling the person who served it to me. Bringing my attention back to my story, I noticed Lokki sitting on the umber leather sofa with the blue boys. People surrounded it, leaving me only a small gap to watch. His popularity knew no limits. He was a magnet that brought in most customers—women and men of all ages. His expression hinted that it didn't bother him. Perhaps he even enjoyed it. Lokki sipped his iced coffee without a care in the world. And all that could be heard from that corner was laughter. Though I looked forward to his arrival, a part of me loathed it. The room changed when he was in it. A warm and comfortable ambiance abruptly changed to a loud and packed one. If I hadn't come so early in the evening, even my corner seat would have been taken. Aside from my mild case of green eyes, I took notice of how different he behaved and how differently he sang. When you see him, you'd think he is a playboy enjoying life, but his lyrics tell otherwise. He spreads words filled with devotion and affection. A thought had crossed my mind, but I quickly erased it. I thought there was a chance someone else wrote the lyrics, maybe a band mate or an acquaintance of his. I brushed it away as my heart begged to differ. When he sang, everything was real. I felt it. Was I nothing but naïve?

I gulped my black coffee and grimaced because of how bitter it was.

The laughter had died down and Lokki, at last, walked to the stage, his band mates following behind. Everyone battled in order to have a seat near the stage. I was content with my seat, even though it was far in the back. His pale slender fingers were placed on the electric guitar he held. Lokki bit his lip and sent out an electrical gaze, making me gulp. With a nod from every player, it began. Normally, I would jot down the lyrics in my memo pad to use as inspiration later on at my pace. Somehow, I couldn't. My hand didn't reach for the pen. It sat on my lap, gripping the end of my shirt. I locked my eyes on his as he sang words that captivated me and almost enchanted me.

"Just as I get used to waiting for you,
You appear like a daydream,
Please enter my meaningless life,

Waking up from my sweet dream,
Every night I pray to the little star watching over me,
I ask the moon to let me see you,
Meet you just like in my dreams,
Oh, I'd run to you."

His gaze on me was cosmic. Why me? Why again? Never did he look away throughout the song and neither did I. I had even forgotten to breathe for a while until my body reminded me of it. The effect of locking eyes with this specimen of a man was inexplicable. You can neither hate it nor love it. You just felt trapped in his cage, without the ability to move or speak. The heart knocked strongly rather than fast. Shoulders rose shyly to the neck and hands turned into a fist. When the last note played, the stage lights dimmed and my human abilities returned so that I could live on. A scoff came out of me. I felt like a fool to have believed, even for a second, that there was a special connection between us. This, without a doubt, was a game he played, and I was just another one of his targets.

I was left with a cold coffee and a blank page. Feeling a little demoralized, I put away my typewriter in its sturdy black case and downed my drink. I was getting ready to leave when I was stopped by a tug on my sleeve.

"You're leaving already, Cosi?" Kylo had said with drooping eyes. That fluffy head of hair added to his canine resemblance.

"Yes, I'm not really finding the words tonight," I truthfully answered.

"It can happen. Will you come again tomorrow?"

"I-" I paused, uncertain of my answer. Tomorrow could be the same as today. My feelings mixed in with work and that was never a good idea.

"Starting tomorrow, to welcome the fall, we are offering pumpkin pie with the purchase of coffee," he said, making me shift perspective.

"I am most definitely coming," a laugh escaped his mouth, and that was it. I was gone without looking back at the set of eyes that I felt watching me from afar.

Chapter 10

Pumpkin pie. The pumpkin pie I'd heard from Kylo last night was taunting me. I wanted to avoid that place at all costs. Whenever I saw Lokki, my heart could not make up its mind. I couldn't bear to be trapped in one of his songs again. It was torture and bliss at the same time. For the pumpkin pie I loved profoundly, not going wasn't an option. Going past the performance was. Lokki came at 10 and left about an hour after. He sang a couple of songs, mingled with the fans and then left, his leather jacket in hand.

I stared at the blazing fire of the fireplace in

my home, waiting for the time to pass. But without realizing it, I had fallen asleep. Relaxed by the warmth, my eyes grew heavy and my body leaned back in the rocking chair.

***

Rain surrounded me, but it did not hit me. I was shielded from it. No umbrella or ceiling covered my head. I was in a circle, in the middle of the street where rain didn't fall. The therapeutic sound made me lower my guard. I stood oblivious to the fact that it was a rather strange occurrence. The night embraced me with its darkness. And slowly, another circle approached mine, one with a person just like me receiving protection. The obscurity had made it near impossible to discern the silhouette standing in front of me.

"Finally," I heard the person say.

"Lips like cherries," I say, opening my eyes. That person in front of me in that dream had lips like cherries. Before I could ask what they meant by finally, it cut away. This dream pleasantly surprised me. My nights were dull without images or scenarios. It had been a long time, though it was odd and rather brief.

Forgetting about it, swiftly, I twisted to the clock. I stood in an instant, letting the rocking chair hit the back of my legs by how abruptly I'd let go of it. The needle was minutes away from reaching midnight. Time suggested that my sleep wasn't as brief as I'd thought. "I must go," I spoke out loud before grabbing the belongings I had left by my feet. The hour was quite late for a lady to be out unattended, but the pumpkin pie called for me. Despite my tooth not being sweet, pumpkin pie was an exception. Precious and long-lasting memories were made with that pie. Someone I loved dearly, often baked it during my younger days. I ran out of the house dramatically at the witching hour with a heavy typewriter for what? A perfect slice of pumpkin pie. Another positive aspect would be the fact that it was certain Lokki had left the place. My complete attention would be on the sweet pastry sitting on a plate. I ran in fear of missing the boat. The coffee shop bar closed late since they did sell alcohol but the pumpkin pie! They wouldn't serve pumpkin pie to people who only wanted to get drunk. And perhaps earlier customers ate it all. I hoped Kylo saved me a slice, but why would he? Thinking I lied. he must have been disappointed and dispirited, and gave away my slice to one of the rainbow ladies.

As I dashed towards the finish line, a drop of water landed on my cheek, startling me. I looked up to see the sudden downpour. Pictures of my dream flashed in my head. Rather strange, this coincidence. Still, it annoyed me, as the day had been sunny, leading me to think it would stay that way until the end. There was an umbrella near the front door, but why pick it up when rain wasn't on the forecast? It would be useless baggage. I was soaking wet with no umbrella or magic circle shielding me. Like I always knew, when you awake from a dream, you face reality. The cold water hit the typewriter case, making a much louder noise than when it fell on the concrete. This sound that was so soothing to me became nothingness. Those empty drops slowed me down a notch. I had found myself walking instead. Perhaps it was for the best. If I slipped and fell, there would be no one to pick me up and make sure I have my slice of pumpkin pie. Excuse my ridiculous words.

 Walking ahead, I noticed the lack of noise and ambiance. Was the sound of the rain too loud to discern any others, or was this night simply dead? My question was soon answered when I arrived. Astounded, my feet came to a halt. At that moment, I only wanted to pinch myself, but I knew I'd look silly and he was the last person I'd wanted to show my silly side to. The coldness and wetness I felt were much too real to think it was a dream. Only steps away from me, Lokki stood. The lead singer of the blue boys and the one I fell for at first sight. He leaned on the closed door of the Cherry street coffee shop bar, legs neatly crossed. Unlike me, he was dry. The roof had covered him. He hadn't noticed me yet. Too shy to mutter a word, I attempted to look through the glass window of the shop with no answers. The inside was dark, and it seemed no one was in.

"The cherry closed early today. There was a water leak," he said, not looking up. Hearing his voice and seeing him up close was something. It was nerve-wracking. Hearing his answer, I should have left in a split second, but I did not. My body stood still, and I clutched my case. At last, he laid his eyes on me. Those already enormous eyes turned wider.

"It's you," he exclaimed, keeping me on my toes. "You weren't here tonight."

"I was occupied," I said, trying to conceal the disappointment in my voice. I suppose he counted his fans, and I was just that for him, a number.

"I was meaning to talk to you," he then added. Did he need my opinion on his songs, or did he need to be showered with compliments?

"What for?"

A corner of his mouth lifted. "First, you must get out of this rain." Lokki walked through the rain, grabbed my wrist and brought me near him, sheltered under the roof. The warmth of his hand on my cold wrist rose to my cheeks, which had gained colour. Lokki proceeded to take off his leather jacket and wrapped me in it. Though I'd read this scene in multiple romance novels, I was afraid of it—with this particular jacket. He wore it every day, and I worried it would reek of sweat. To my pleasant surprise, the only scent there was, was lemon scented fabric softener. The sensible guy who sang those love songs had come back to me. Maybe he never left. Lokki grabbed my wrist once again. "I know a secret way to the Cherry." He said, running down the narrow path separating us from the rain.

I let myself be dragged away for the sole

reason that curiosity was eating me alive. I wanted to have at least one conversation with him. This was my love language, conversations. We arrived at what seemed to simply be the back of the shop, brick walls and a worn down metal door. He bent down to take a key from under a flowerpot that looked to be out of place. Still wrapping his lean fingers around my wrist, he stepped a foot inside. It was dark, but I followed.

"Be careful of your step," he told me.

A cramped staircase had presented itself with the opening of the door. We stuck together and climbed, my heart rate climbing faster. It was so quiet that I gained consciousness of my breath and could hear it as if a megaphone amplified it. Step after step, my mind drifted. Many thoughts should have come to me at such a moment. I should have been the least bit concerned by his acts. I should have wondered where exactly he was bringing me since I'd never needed to take a flight of stairs to enter the *Cherry,* as he called it. I was mindless and over-trusting. My heart had taken over the brain, leaving no space for negotiations.

"We're here."

"Where is here?" I replied, unsure of what he meant when darkness filled a room that seemed to be almost entirely void with the exception of a couple of cardboard boxes at the edge. The floor looked grey, either from dust or lights reflected from the glass doors, lightening the blackness of it.

"It's my fort, one could also call it a secret base." *Childish-much*, I thought.

Lokki brought me near the closed glass doors. From there, we had a blurred view of Cherry street. Rain transported by the wind hit the glass, permitting us to only see colourful orbs of light. "I would open the doors and let you observe the night sky from the balcony, but I am afraid it wouldn't be wise." We were out of luck. Clouds covered the sky, leaving us searching for a hole to discern at least a single star. He crouched to take a seat on the floor facing the view and tapped next to him, motioning me to do the same.

"It's truly mesmerizing. I simply don't understand why you've brought me up here," I said, afraid I'd stepped into his game. Perhaps he brought others before me. It was part of his plan, to charm the lady with an amazing view and...

He raised an eyebrow. "I'll give you the explanation you deserve if you give me time to."

"The stage is yours," I said, sitting on the floor slightly farther away from him, my hair dripping on the floor, forming small puddles. These words of mine resembled a cue that made every performer nervous, including the charismatic looking Lokki. Without his leather jacket, he seemed a timid boy fiddling with his fingers, trying to get a sound out.

"I have dreams, strange but enjoyable ones. In those dreams, there is a pair of green eyes." he focused on the eyes that were locked on him. "More precisely, they're moss-green eyes and I'd recognize them anywhere." I held my breath and asked for my brain to co-operate for a second. His lines were honeyed, just like that face of his. How many had he charmed with a single look? When he opens that mouth of his, many certainly would have died—their heart rate coming to a halt.

"I'll need more than this."

"I like you." Though I had an inkling of a crush on him, this sudden confession was abysmal.

"How is it you like me? You don't know me. Have you only fallen for my eyes? Perhaps you could put a price on them and I'll tell you I'll consider your offer."

He laughed, the sound tickling my ears. "I still have a bit of explaining to do."

I turned around facing the coloured light orbs following the raindrops drooping down the glass, leaving a watered line.

"You might think I'm crazy. I do myself, but this truth cannot be denied. For a long time now, I've seen a mysterious lady in dreams. Day by day, love grew in me. Even if that girl might have been an illusion, I kept my heart open for the day I'd meet her." Sincerity filled his voice and had me want to believe in his whimsical words.

"How can you be so sure it's me? I cannot be the only person with green eyes in Mardi Town."

"Nobody in this town or in the world has these eyes of yours," he quickly retorted. "There is one thing that could prove our connection. I reckon it's worth a try."

He placed a hand forth, waiting for another to be placed on top. With arched eyebrows, a lower lip sticking out and sparkling eyes staring deeply into mine, it was hard to refuse. Indeed, I laid my hand. Once he intertwined his fingers with mine, everything went colourful. Ladies and gentlemen, I present to you "Epiphany" with its special guests: Butterflies.

Chapter 11

I was overwhelmed. I shut my eyes and observed a view that was far from pitch black. Stars all around me, shining bright as ever. Moonlight lifting my heart, letting it slide down the lengthy milky way. Warmth from the radiant lights, invading my body. These little blue butterflies carried me to where I belonged, faintly kissing my hand, leaving it tingling.

"What are these cosmic feelings?" I muttered under my breath.

"They are the same ones I felt and am still feeling every time I see you," he replied, making me open my eyes. I had seen him in a new light. The day he entered the Cherry making me turn my head, I was attracted, but it was purely physical, I think. Upon hearing his songs, I fell a little deeper. Seeing the immense attention he received made me want to move on. And I thought it'd be easy since we hadn't exchanged words with each other. Little did I know those songs were meant for my ears to hear. The lyrics sang with emotion were mine and so was this hand I held. This new spiritual attraction hadn't felt so new. With a touch, I was reunited with a long-lost lover.

Stupefied, I smiled. "The universe is truly a mystery."

"You know it, milady," he told me before bringing my hand near his lips and leaving a tender kiss on it. There I was swept by a high tide called love.

***

The night seemed never-ending. We talked for so long my hair had already dried. We discussed our lives, our preferences and a couple of fun facts. It was insane to be able to open up in such a short and sweet time. This was not the way it usually happened. It's almost as if it wasn't our first conversation. And I was wrong about Lokki. He was sweet and always listened without judgment. Even if we'd sometimes have differences, he'd wear my eyes and try to watch the world from my perspective.

"Fun fact," Lokki began.

"Hit me."

"My grandfather chose my name, and it's a Finnish one."

"Oh, are you Finnish or have family there?"

"Not at all!" He laughed, the corner of his eyes crinkling. "Neither I nor my grandfather have an ounce of Finish blood in us, he simply loved seagulls and the Finish word for seagull is Lokki. Out of all the other translations, he preferred this one. It is simple but quite comic, don't you think?"

"Yes, his love for seagulls is as unique as your name." He observed me in a certain way, attentively. His eyes always turned to me when I spoke. Rather than being charmed, I felt loved.

"Fun fact," I said without thinking of one ahead. We'd share so much, I don't think I had any fun facts left. I pursed my lips in defeat.

"Already out of fun facts, Cosi?" He had shortened my name as soon as he heard it.

"I cannot help it. I've lived a dull life."

"Do not worry. Life is about to get colourful," he said, adjusting the leather jacket on my shoulders making sure it fully wrapped me.

Colourful. It was a wish of mine to have such a life. Was he a soulmate or a genie? Did I have two more wishes and was he to disappear after having fulfilled them?

"I need to ask you something," he said, sitting straight up.

"Yes?"

"Would you like to accompany me to a ball tomorrow night?" Lokki pressed his lips together, eyes round and nervous.

"Tomorrow night?"

"Well, actually tonight, it seems the sun will rise any minute now."

My usual self would have said that I didn't go to balls nor did I have an elegant dress to attend, but a voice inside me told me to take in the colours. And so...

"I'll gladly accompany you, Lokki."

There it was, his hearty smile, the one that only I could witness. I'm sure he hadn't shown that much teeth to others at the *Cherry*.

"Great, I'll pick you up at 7:30. I wouldn't let a lady walk alone at night searching for a ballroom."

"This lady walked by herself at night to get here, but sure, I'll wait for you." I was proud, sometimes fearless, that's because I had no choice but to be independent quite early on. In front of this man, though, I toned it down. I wanted to see him again, and the sooner, the better.

***

I hated the sun. It was rising in the corner of our eyes. We both knew it was time to leave, but our hesitant eyes were fixed on each other —occasionally trailing elsewhere but coming back, eventually. We spoke with glances rather than words, sad that these words would be farewells. The blade had to cut.

"It would be nice to get some sleep before the big day ahead of us," I said, removing the jacket from my back, folding it neatly. He reached his hands out to take it back. I stopped in the process of handing it to him. It wasn't that I was reluctant to give away the jacket. Not at all. It's just shivers. When his warm skin touched my ice-cold skin, it felt good.

"Are your hands always this cold?" he asked me, holding them under the jacket.

"I'm afraid so. Are yours always this warm?" I asked, not thinking much before speaking, once again. So it was true, love changes people. I don't know if for the better or worst. Your character completely changes.

He looked down, smiling, "My hands and their warmth are yours." That reply had almost made me barf—I tried not to by sheepishly smiling. In due time, Lokki caught on and grimaced. We laughed at our silliness, and with difficulty, parted ways. He went to the right side of the street and I pretended to go on the left while I watched him walk away. It was a bitter-sweet moment. Once I couldn't even see the heel of his shoes, it would be my turn to walk away. The grumbling of my stomach interrupted the sad farewells. I'd missed dinner last night because of having taken a nap. Standing at the crossroads, I thought it technically was already time for breakfast. Daylight covered Cherry street, birds sang their morning song, and the breeze was strong enough to bring a sweet pumpkin scent near my nose.

Oh, please don't let this be a hallucination, I thought, making my way to the source of this delicious scent.

To my surprise, it came from the Cherry. That is right, I am officially calling it the Cherry now, not because I wanted to be cool like Lokki but because it was quicker to say.

To my other surprise, the lights were turned on at the shop. My hunger and curiosity joined forces and walked me to the door. Full of expectations, I knocked—gently since the hour was early. My nose moved on its own, sniffing the spices of a pumpkin pie I'd recognize just came out of the oven.

At last, a bare arm twisted the knob. Looking up, I saw Bruno, his head tilted on the side.

"Cosi?"

"Are you open for breakfast?" I had wasted no time getting to the point. I was a lion smelling the meat.

"We still have plumbing issues, but you are welcome in. I'll find a way to serve you breakfast."

"Oh, I don't mean to bother you. A simple

slice of pumpkin pie is sufficient." My tongue had gotten shorter and the volume of my voice lower by the end of that sentence.

"That, I can do with no problem."

Hearing his approval, I rushed past him—making the unbuttoned end of his blue stripped shirt fly a little.

Both elbows were on the table as my head rested on the palms of my hands. Drowsiness came, bringing me into a daze. The past hours flew through my head. Unconsciously, my lips lifted higher by the second. The sound of a plate hitting the table snapped me out of the daze.

"Something nice must have happened," Kylo remarked.

"It's nothing really," I tried containing the smile threatening to escape. Of course, due to my lack of sleep, I couldn't. Euphoria took over me and said it will never let go.

"There must be something. You haven't stopped by last night, even when you said you'd do. And now, I find you in the shop grinning at five in the morning." He sat in front of me, trying to pinpoint the meaning of my smile. I wished he'd get off my case.

"I'm sorry for that. I tried to come, but the

cherry closed early."

"It closed at 11:30. You used to come hours before that."

"I wanted it to do things differently." *Excuses.* "No promises were broken," I continued explaining, showing down the delightful pie.

"What about this morning? Why are you here this early?" This interrogation changed my image of him. He went from golden retriever to parrot, who has too much to say. Perhaps he should join the rainbow ladies in their talks—they were missing a colour.

"I couldn't sleep," *I lied.*

It would have been fun to talk to someone about my little escapade with Lokki, but Kylo wasn't right for it. Truly, it was a shame I couldn't speak about it. Even if we'd been more friendly towards each other, I wouldn't dare to tell him I trespassed the property. Would I?

Kylo endlessly flapped his tongue for at least thirty minutes more until I'd excuse myself, saying I had to get some sleep. I kept hearing his voice on the way back as if he were next to me. It was haunting. Lokki had talked a lot as well, but our conversation was mutual. Every word coming out of his mouth was a kiss on the ear. Lokki was and will always be a heart shaker.

One inch closer. The slowly moving clock needle was one inch closer to the time Lokki knocked on my door. After having been re-energized from a needed slumber, I used my remaining time to doll myself up. I haven't done that in ages or perhaps, ever. With great difficulty, I'd found an appropriate dress. It was one I wore for a high-class party I attended for work purposes. They'd let me keep the dress, as it was the least expensive part of the ensemble. I've done odd jobs—nothing inappropriate—I was fortunate enough to find these good but odd small jobs.

The dress that was hidden in the back of my closet was, even to me, sublime. It was pine green and made of velvet. The dress covered my body from top to bottom, revealing only my collarbone, a few centimetres of my ankles and my arms excluding the shoulder, who were covered by slightly puffed sleeves in a darker shade of green. There wasn't much detail to it other than a couple of creases on the skirt and depth at the waist. It was comfortable to wear and didn't hinder me the least with useless lace or extra ruffles. I did not own pearls, gold bracelets or a diamond ring, thus my hair was down, hoping it could cover my bare neck. It mattered little. My intention wasn't to stand out, it was merely to spend an enjoyable evening.

Looking at myself on the glass, I feared the worst. I feared he would be disappointed or embarrassed. Perhaps he'll keep his distance from me in the ball for no one to think I accompanied him. Here came my inner devil. Lokki didn't seem to be a person who would be affected by the regards of other people. For once, I was right. When I had opened the door to face him, his expression was nowhere near the one my devil drew in my mind. And I knew the person in front of me was perfect when I saw his leather jacket covering the traditional black tuxedo he wore. He held his black bow tie with his thumb and index finger while he stared at me for a while. I did the same until it came to my attention. We were standing in different places. Though the door was open, it still separated us.

"I would let you in, but the house is a mess. Why don't we get on the road?" I proposed, closing the door behind me.

He coughed. "It wouldn't hurt to be a little late. I need more time to look."

Flustered by his words, I gripped on the skirt, lips fighting a smile. He stared and I... couldn't take it. My cheeks were flaming. It wasn't fair. I had also wanted to take my time observing how good he looked, but how could I with such intense eyes on me?

"Well, good evening," I said out of the blue, noticing we hadn't exchanged greetings.

"Good evening," a grin plastered on his face. "You look beautiful tonight. I'm sorry it took so long to tell you. Oh, and I only brought my jacket in case you'd come out dressed this way having no fear of the cold."

He removed the jacket from his shoulders

and placed it on mine. The butterflies returned, and they outnumbered me—they'd invited their friends and held a ball of their own.

"It's nice of you, but won't you be cold?"

"I'll be fine."

Lokki gave me a special smile, one I loved with passion. The corners of his mouth curved more upwards rather than sideways and his eyes gleamed. It was a warm cup of milk.

"Shall we go now?" I had repeated.

"We shall, my dear." He reached a hand out, maintaining that warm cup of milk smile. We walked hand in hand throughout the streets of Mardi Town. We passed Cherry street not looking at the road itself but each other. It was heart fluttering, really. I'd turn his way, catching him staring, and he'd look away. I would watch our hands and he'd squeeze it oh so gently. I skipped away happily, not caring what would happen to my cheap black low heels, and he'd skip along humming sweet melodies. We were children again, blinded by the streetlights. For a split second, in the corner of my eye, I had caught a glimpse of Kylo's blue eyes peering out the window of the Cherry but had ignored it. My eyes were fixed on a single sight, one I couldn't believe was near me.

"Is it long before we arrive?" I wasn't being impatient, in contrary, I wished the road ahead would be long. I'd much rather wander the town with Lokki at my side than attending a party with people of a much higher class than I'll ever be.

"We're nearing it, but we don't need to rush. It is nice taking our sweet time."

"Yes, it is. Tell me Lokki," I started.

"I'll tell you everything you want to hear."

With a chuckle, I inquired, "Why is it you are bringing me to this ball?" My fears hadn't entirely dissipated. "Maybe you've realized, but I'm not one to waltz regularly and you don't look much of an amuse-bouche eater either."

"You're right. In fact, I've never attended a ball." My curiosity grew. "It all started with a dream. I dreamt we were dancing in the centre of a ballroom. In a certain dark time of my life, those dreams were my newly found *joie de vivre*. I based my songs on this connection we have. Though I cannot remember our past, I am sure that this feeling I have in my heart is mutual."

"Oh yes it is," I quickly said, with an inexplicable urge. I bit my lip and stopped in tracks. "I've never believed in destiny or hope itself, but when I'm with you, I feel like even pigs could fly."

His free hand rested on my cheek—the touch, a fire on ice. Closing his eyes, he leaned until not even air separated us. And then it happened. His lips touched mine. I pressed mine on his ever so gently. Cosmic feelings had struck again. We were two stars orbiting the same point, and we colluded, creating an explosion. Space was filled with the colourful and shining debris. I was fed memories of my companion star. Images flew right past me, one being a dance we shared at the ball and one being a tear dropping out of my eye. After what was the first kiss I'd always dreamed of having, my mind wandered to that last image. I had the bad feeling it was all too good to be true, and that reality had never been this kind. Seeing the sudden worry in his eyes, I brushed it off. If we were to live as Romeo and Juliet, let us enjoy our time. I threw my arms around his waist and buried my head in his chest. A pair of arms welcomed me into an embrace. Never will I forget the warmth that no teddy bear could ever give me.

"I remember," I told him, listening to his unsteady heartbeat.

"What do you remember?"

"When we kissed, I briefly saw what you had seen during your sleep. Images," I hadn't mentioned the particular image that perhaps only I had seen.

In surprise, he stretched his arms, pulling me back and stared with big fish eyes. Whenever he widened his eyes, to me it only resembled fish's. "This just confirms the magic surrounding us!"

Lokki pulled out of his pocket a crumpled invitation, receiving a glare from the security guard whose hands had become delicate when reaching for it. Another employee tried to take away his leather jacket when I intervened.

"Shouldn't we bring it along with us? It looks to be precious."

"It won't be stolen here. You can let the man take it away. He'll give it back when we leave."

"Alright then," I gave away the jacket, feeling apologetic to the man who was just doing his work.

Music had already started. The sound of trumpets and violins filled the room. Musicians passionately played while people danced along on the dance floor. The number of individuals breathing the same air overwhelmed me. Lokki had probably sensed my discomfort and grabbed my hand. Talking with eyes, he'd tell me he's by my side.

"What are we supposed to do in a ball?" I asked, oblivious as well as out of my mind.

"We dance," he said, dragging me to the centre of the floor.

"But we just arrived. Shouldn't we mingle and talk about the funny character we'd just met and get offered a cocktail by a waiter wearing a bow tie just like yours?"

"Perhaps we'll do all of this later. I only came to share a dance with you. Would you give me the honours?"

I stroked my chin, pretending hesitation was on my mind, but for the life of me, I couldn't act. He raised our already intertwined hands and place a hand on my waist while I placed mine on his shoulder.

"I have to be honest with you. I am not much of a dancer. I'm giving you the chance to retreat before being humiliated in front of everyone."

"Follow my steps, the music in your ears and you'll be fine." Just as he said, it was fine, or maybe more than fine. We swayed here and there, taking over the dance floor. People watched not because I stepped on his shoes but because we had rhythm. We followed every note and forgot about the people we shared air with. We were two love birds waltzing in an empty ballroom.

"You know, sometimes, I feel the moon sent me to you, Cosi," Lokki said, getting a hold of me after a twirl.

"Why is that?"

"Well, I prayed to the moon every night to let me see you, the girl of my dreams and darling. Now, all I want to do is chase those beautiful dreams with you." All I could do was laugh and slow dance. The music had slowed down much more and our bodies had gotten closer. We stood on a single tile and swayed right to left, still following the musical notes. He held his dazzling gaze on me and opened his mouth once again to say another cheesy line.

"You know, there is something else I wanted to tell you."

"What again?"

"There was no sunshine where I was before-"

"Let me finish this one for you, and now you're walking on sunshine, right?"

"Your version is better than what I had in mind. Perhaps I'll need your help for lyrics."

"And what was the original?" He twirled me to the next tile in order to avoid answering. "I am dying of curiosity," I said, regaining my balance.

"Speaking of lyrics, I've written new songs, and I'd love for you to hear them. I'll be playing them tomorrow night at the Cherry."

"I cannot wait," his songs fascinated me and his voice... Oh I loved his honey voice, All I wanted was to hear him sing. "Can't you sing something to me, only me, before tomorrow night?"

"Right now? Right here?" he looked at me as if I was crazy and who could blame him?

"Of course not. We could slip out of the ball, find a cozy tree outside, sit under it, and then you could sing one of your sweet songs. Oh, please, I couldn't hear you sing last night. Let's not make it two nights in a row."

He gave in with a smile, the kind I liked. "I

suppose we could do that." Still dancing, we discreetly made our way out. We found a door near the table of hors d'oeuvres and escaped. It was too dark to see anything. I walked, not knowing if we were going to bump into that cozy tree of ours.

"We don't necessarily need to find a tree," I remarked, impatient to hear his voice. Even the sound of his laughter made my heart play the drums. He held both of my hands and though I could not see him, I was sure he'd be looking at me.

"I truly love you," he said, making me teary-eyed. It once again felt too good to be true. There was a man in front of me I loved who was telling me he loved me just as much. A first love could never be this special.

"I love you too."

He stroked my hands with his thumbs and took a deep breath—I had held mine. The silent before he sang was loud, tense and sounded almost ominous.

"I thought it was all a dream,
You looked at me with those lovely eyes,
You made me breathless,
My heart stopped,
And now I tell you I love-" He stopped.

The silence was much louder. His grip on my hands loosened. His hands had lost mine. The sound of his breath was gone and then followed a big thud.

"I'm sorry, Cosi." I heard, but it was not his voice. At that moment, I didn't realize what had just happened. The rustling of grass brought me back to my senses.

"What are you sorry for?"

"The dead man on the grass." My heart dropped, I dropped on my knees scattering to get a hold of Lokki. There was indeed a body on the floor, a still one with a still heart. It killed me that I could not see him. There was not even a single light. I could only touch his body, whose temperature dropped by the second. How could this be? In an instant, without a sound. Shock took its place in me and stole my voice, my tears and my head, who turned blank.

"A vital spot is all it took," the man whose voice I now recognized said. A blood thirst I never had awakened in me. It didn't matter if the blood reached my hands for killing him. I'd done it without hesitation. But I didn't. I laid on Lokki and held him tight. His dress shirt soaked in tears—making my eyes a desert.

This was truly a ballroom extravaganza.

***

After spending days with insanity, I made a choice, one I should have made that very night.

The guilt had driven me insane. If we had stayed in the ballroom, we would've headed home—hands in each other. And tonight, he'd sing again.

He won't sing anymore. Lokki and the blue boys wouldn't perform those new songs and I'd never get the chance to hear them. I don't see how I could live anymore knowing he's not here. It all felt like a fever dream. Perhaps it was. I followed another dream. One many writers shared. To die on their typewriter.

Chapter 14

Sol's point of view

      I was a weeping, broken mess. The last page of the manuscript had personally ripped my heart out. I could not mutter a word and neither could Eugene, who let a couple of tears escape himself. We sat at our table near the window and spent hour after hour reading the manuscript we'd—by miracle—uncovered from under a tree. Thankfully, Cosi had wrapped it in plastic making it spotless when taking it out.

Night had fallen and there were fewer people

—many have come and go.

"That was quite the ride," I told him in a breathy voice.

"Indeed, but... We meet again."

A sudden rush of happiness rose, and I fought the urge to throw myself at him. For a slight second, I felt the Cosi in me reuniting with her Lokki. He didn't feel like so much of a stranger now.

"In a way, I suppose we did meet again."

Despite having seen old pictures of our lookalikes and having felt Cosi's emotions as my own, I had a hard time believing. Just like Cosi, I thought of it as a fever dream. However, I came to the conclusion that it was worth a try. I'd regret it if I'd left myself wondering *what if...*

Mustering some courage, I confessed the strange dreams I'd previously had in order to take a step ahead. The dreams seemed to be a key piece to this mess of a puzzle laid on our hands.

"I'm pretty sure you're that hoodie boy. You even smell like lemon. I should've known it was you the first time I heard your voice. I'm sorry."

I've smelt the sweet lemon fragrance on

him this morning. Last night, I suppose the candle scent had been too strong to notice his. As for his voice, my ears had been deaf. How did that honey voice not ring a bell?

"You don't need to apologize. Besides, black hoodies are much more common than moss-green eyes. Lokki had it easier than you."

"Isn't it weird how we switched roles? You were supposed to have the dreams, and I just needed to look pretty until you approached me."

"The second part hasn't changed, has it?" he said, a smirk shaping itself on his face.

"You really are Lokki," I didn't let his smirk get to me and I certainly couldn't lose either.

"Yes, we both have cheesy lines in our pockets and like to wear black clothes."

It hit me.

"Speaking of black clothes. Do you think Cosi took back the leather jacket from that employee, or would it be lost forever?" Without even having seen this leather jacket, I was attached to it. The Cosi in me would have wanted to have it over her shoulders.

"She didn't mention it in the manuscript."

"It would be crazy to try to find it, right? I mean, we only know it's a leather jacket and there are millions of them, right? We could never pull it off," I said with a hint of sarcasm and seriousness. I glanced at him warily every time I said: Right?

"I'd love to try. Maybe tomorrow, because have you seen the time? The moon is up and the *Cherry* is closing soon."

No lie there. Time today passed like we were in Saturn, where days are merely eleven hours long.

"Alright, then give me your number." *Did I say that?* "Uh, we'll see each other again tomorrow morning. It's just in case one of us has a breakthrough in the middle of the night or something like that." I quickly made up an excuse and quickly realized I should've said that part first.

"You don't even need to ask," he said, taking a phone out of the pocket of his sweat pants.

Well, that's a little stupid of him. I didn't really ask. I *told* him to give me his number. This time, I didn't laugh by myself, but openly with someone who followed along.

Eugene removed the hood from his head, revealing a silky head of hair, and I could now properly see him. He's pretty good looking.

How did I ever glue my eyes to a manuscript for hours when he was sitting beside me?

"Is something on my face?" he said, staring just as much as I did—except his stare was more playful.

"Aren't you comic to use the same line I used yesterday?"

"Maybe."

That's it, the magic happened to us too. Cosi's butterflies migrated to my stomach. I wonder what Eugene was feeling during our never ending eye contact. It's not because our doppelgangers fell in love that we will too. I mean, maybe I am falling in love, but how can I be so sure? And how do I know he is too? My mind was as confused as the people still trying to figure out the string theory.

"Um, we're closing," Bruno said, creeping from behind.

He broke our trance and startled me.

"Right, we better leave." I stood, strapping my bag to my shoulders.

We walked out of the *Cherry* and both took on the habit of calling it the Cherry. Why didn't we think of it sooner? Lokki truly was effortlessly cool.

"There's so much we haven't discussed

after having read the manuscript," he said, and it reassured me to know that at least this feeling was mutual.

"There is, but if we did, I don't think we'll have even a wink of sleep tonight and trust me, we need many winks."

The story emotionally drained me, and my eyes were barely holding up.

"I'm dead tired," he added, slouching to show just how much he was dead on his feet. Laughter never ended when we were together. I take it as a good sign.

"I'll walk you home," he started. "It's late for you to be out."

"This lady can-" *pause*, "but would not walk alone at this hour, thank you."

"No problem, even for me it would be scary."

"Oh, then would you like me to walk you home?"

"I did martial arts as a hobby in the town I previously lived in, so I'm okay, but thanks."

I don't know if this conversation was a joke or if we really were being honest. I can barely recall, we were fatigued. The only thing I could remember was having the urge to hold his hand and walk like Cosi and Lokki did. The

2020s were not as romantic as the 30s. If I took his hand, I'd look and feel like a creep. Regardless of our so-called soul connection, there were boundaries and lines to not cross and so I used our remaining time doing the only thing I could do: talk. I did my best avoiding the manuscript topic since I needed for this day to end. I couldn't think of something that wasn't related to the past because it was the only thing we could relate to.

"Eugene?"

"Yes?"

"Would you mind telling me about how you've found your passion as a photographer?"

"Are you still worried about your future?"

"How couldn't I? I'm an adult with no plan."

"That's a rite of passage. You're on a crossroad not knowing which direction to choose." He'd stopped walking and looked me deep in the eye. "One day, you'll cross. No matter what."

I wasn't used to moments of this sort. It felt good and terrifying, simultaneously. The confidence in his words went right down my spine and up again to rattle inside my brain. I had to ease this tense yet warm air surrounding us.

"That talk of crossing makes me think of death. You know how they say when someone dies, they crossed."

"I shouldn't be laughing, but yes, it *crossed* my mind as well." That's it, we exploded. We were morbid, laughing about death.

Being with Eugene brought a character I didn't know was in me. I was never morbid or witty, only plain boring.

He continued, "All I really wanted to say is that I'm sure you'll find a passion that will burn your heart."

"That sounds painful."

"It is. Liking your job doesn't mean rolling in sunshine and rainbows every day."

"Thank you for being realistic and not feeding me pipe dreams."

"I hope I wasn't too pessimist and discouraged you."

"No, no. don't worry. I prefer to walk with open eyes." I gave an upward-curving smile, only to have it mirrored by him.

"I think we'll get along *just* fine," he said, elongating the *just*.

He read my mind, and I was in my déjà vu.

Not only did walking at night together feel familiar, but it was. We had proof.

It saddened me that my house was so close to the Cherry. We were already here. I gave my back to the front door and had a last look at the marvel that was Eugene. The silky hair coming out of his hood, the eyes reflecting on the streetlights and the overall *warm cup of milk* aura he sent out.

"I'll see you tomorrow," I said, reluctant to enter the house. Now that I was this close to him, I didn't want to be apart or at a distance. The conclusion of Cosi and Lokki's story scared me. They had little time together after they finally talked. These thoughts triggered a ticking bomb in my head. There was no saying when it would explode, ending our story. Without consent, a tear slipped from my right eye, making Eugene frown.

"What's wrong?" He went ahead and placed his hands on my shoulders.

"Nothing," I first said, not realizing my chances of speaking could become limited. With our fate, any time, could be the last. "You're going to think I'm crazy, but I'm scared. Scared that our time is as limited as theirs was."

He gently squeezed my shoulders, his features softening. "We deserve a happy ending this time and I'll make sure it happens even if I need to wear a bulletproof or knife-proof vest. I won't disappear on you instantly and we'll live to be very old people complaining every day about how we've had enough of this life."

His humour was right up my alley. It reached my heart and comforted me. Man, was I a strange person to be comforted by words like these? We are freaks. What can I say? We said our goodbyes, and I tried my utmost best to not wake my parents, who would be asleep by now. I collapsed on my bed, thinking that for once, I looked forward to the unpredictable tomorrow.

Eugene's point of view

I fiddled, paced around the living room all while trying to keep my bed hair down. Should I? Should I not? I spent minutes after minute concerning myself with a single button, the *'send'* one. I was about to send Sol a message saying something simple like "good morning". in the middle of typing, my brain started to fry—in other words: over-think. We'd meet soon, anyway. If the message was sent, I'd need to greet her twice. Weird, no? In the end, I deleted the words on the text box and went on with my morning. I was still in a daze and, to be honest, my sleep wasn't great. My night was filled with memories, hazy ones. The manuscript was in Sol's hands, but I attempted to imagine the scenes I remembered reading. It was easy to envision since I resembled Lokki and she Cosi. I could just picture Sol in that pine green dress that would bring out her eyes and strangely, I could see myself holding a microphone and singing at the Cherry. It helped that there was a picture of that scene. The hard-to-believe concept of reincarnation and soul mates haunted my mind. Questions filled my fried mind and I couldn't take it any longer. Grabbing the bag I hadn't unpacked the night before, I went to the Cherry.

My first sight there was Sol waving at me from our seat—looking as hypnotizing as ever.

"Good morning," she said.

"Good morning, Sol."

"How many winks of sleep did you get?"

"Just as much as you did."

"That few, huh?" Our conversations flowed so easily. They were casual interactions I dreamed of—two people with a similar humour throwing small jokes here and there.

"Did you order something yet?"

"No, I was waiting for you," she told me, making her way to the counter.

"Hello, Sol!" Bruno exclaimed, displaying a huge grin that disappeared as soon as he laid eyes on me. I was catching up on the whole Bruno situation and I now know why is it he treated me so differently. He has a thing for Sol and I'm the threat. The grin teleported itself on my face, becoming larger on the way.

"Hello, Bruno," I said, sticking closer to Sol. "We'd like to order," I continued, very clearly saying: "*We*".

I saw a new expression on Bruno's face. He was dumbfounded. Fumes came out of his ears. How I wanted to laugh, but that would be childish.

"A cold brew for me and..." She turned her head towards me.

"A dark roast."

"Coming right up," he said, pressing or should I say crushing the buttons of the cash register.

"What's wrong with him?" she whispered to me on our way back.

"What isn't wrong with him?" this line I was

proud of earned me a chuckle.

Sitting properly, I jumped to the subject we've all been waiting for.

"Shall we talk about the manuscript? Honestly, it's driving me crazy."

"Tell something I don't know," she replied with the type of sarcasm I loved.

"Alright, what do we start with? There's so much to talk about."

"Why don't we start with reincarnation?"

"Sure, do you believe in it?" I asked, curious about her point of view.

"I didn't, but seeing these pictures and reading the manuscript, I'm not so sure," she paused for a moment, "There is something that's troubling me about it."

"What is it?"

"From what I've read on reincarnation last night, because, hey, a few winks of sleep but hours of free time, right?"

"Right."

"Well, souls reincarnate in other bodies and so they should look completely different."

"I thought of that too."

"We could just have doppelgangers, but what are the odds of being re-born in them as well as meeting in the same exact place?"

"Maybe, and I say maybe we're vampires with amnesia," I said before we both got a headache.

"That's a possibility," Sol said, tilting her head.

"The coffee's ready..." we heard a grumbling from behind. It was Bruno who wore his emotions on his sleeves.

"There's really something wrong with him today," Sol said, oblivious to the situation.

"Maybe he woke up on the wrong side of the bed?" Another chuckle in the bank and I was over the moon.

"Here, rather than to focus on the present, let's go back to the past and dissect this manuscript a bit," she suggested, bringing it out of her bag.

"What I want to know most is who killed Lokki."

"Right. It tormented me all night."

"Cosi said she knew him."

Flipping through the olden pages, she spoke: "I do have someone in mind, but it's a wild guess, with no proof whatsoever."

"Shoot."

"Kylo. He's the only other man that was mentioned in the book, and it seems he had a little thing for Cosi."

Oh, Sol, you caught that, but not the Bruno situation?

"I had this suspect in mind, but like you said, there's no proof. It would be hard to find anything now."

"Very hard. I think we were lucky to find this manuscript, but that's where we may run out of luck. Any chance you feel you've used up all your luck recently? Hopefully not. Let's save a little luck for the leather jacket."

I couldn't answer her silly question because I did feel like I had used up all my luck recently.

"We'll find the jacket." I truly wanted that for her.

"I hope so."

And again, our eyes locked. It's always hard to get out of these moss-green eyes. My lips just curved up like that, without even asking first. How rude. Her eyes were like the solar eclipse you weren't supposed to watch bare-eyed or else you'll be blinded for life. In this case, you'd be blind to everything but her.

Seeing the thin steam coming out of my coffee prompted me to drink it before it cooled down. Sol was fortunate not to have this problem. They served her coffee cold. That reminded of something I had to lie on the table:

"Isn't it funny that I drink warm coffee and you drink cold coffee while it was the other way around in the manuscript?"

"It's a minor detail, yes. I wonder what statement the universe was trying to give with that."

"Maybe the universe has a sense of humour?"

"That or we're digging too deep."

"I don't know where to dig anymore."

"The ballroom? Why don't we try to find the ballroom?" she suggested.

"That would be a start."

"Alright, the only clue we have is that it was at a walking distance from here."

"Are you enunciating we should walk Cherry street and a couple of streets near in search of a ballroom?"

"No, silly," she gave me a look I've grown fond of—lowered eyes and pouted lips. "We first have to consider the possibility of it not being a ballroom anymore. Actually, it's likely since there are no balls anymore."

"Maybe not balls, but events. With a room this big, they could use it for cocktail events or something like that." it was obvious that I knew little about events.

"You have a point, mister!" Her entire face lightened up.

"I do?" Now I just sounded dumb.

"Let's use these machines of ours that Cosi could've used to write her novels if she had access to them," Sol said, making me rack my brain. "Laptops," she added since I was looking at her in a clueless way.

"Oh, yes, these machines," I said, taking it out of my bag. "We could easily research what's nearby on the map. You know, we could also ask Bruno. He knew about the pictures."

"I guess..." she said, dropping her shoulders—dragging each and every feature of her face along.

"Or not. We can research first." It was fascinating to watch her change expression—not even in a complete second—her cheekbones grew and the corner of her eyes almost reached those cheekbones. "You know, the more I see you, the more it feels familiar.

Did we meet in a previous life or something?" I said, laughing a bit.

I thought she would laugh too, but no, she lightly hit my arm.

"There's no time for jokes. Focus on the research," she said, attempting to hide a mischievous smile. Sol could not hide things. It eventually shown itself on her face. Her eyes talked to me, the edges of her lips and the movement of her eyebrows. It was all fairly easy to read, at least for me. Maybe we've just gotten close, or we always were. I was really starting to believe in the concept of soul connections.

"Oh! I found something. There's a party venue near called Aveberry events."

"How near?"

"Ten minutes near."

"I'm ready to go. What about you? Don't you have to study?"

"I couldn't care less about these lessons I study without an apparent reason. What about *you*? You like your work." My heart broke a little, hearing her talk. I've always had this passion of mine and couldn't imagine living without one. It happened before, to have had doubts about my career choice, but they never brought me to the point of giving up, only the edge.

"I do like my job but I also..." I almost blurted out something I shouldn't have. "I have time to spare. So I guess we're out of here," I ended, downing the rest of my coffee.

I hoped for Sol to find the work she couldn't take her eyes off.

***

"In 10 meters, turn to your right to Berry street," the robotic lady voice said from the GPS on Sol's phone.

"I think I'm gonna mute this. We can read while walking," Sol said, angrily pressing the volume button on the side of her phone. I was glad she did—the voice annoyed me as well.

The gravel underneath our feet had been wet from the rain we hadn't noticed came. An autumn-like breeze constantly hit on us, bringing Sol to rub her arms that were covered by a thin sky blue shirt. Following my instincts, I took off my hoodie and handed it to her.

"Oh no," she frowned. "You should keep it on or you'll be the one to freeze."

"So be it," I replied, putting it on her using minimal force.

Once her head stuck out the hoodie with now dishevelled hair, she stated,

"Déjà vu."

"You're right, it also feels like a déjà vu for me."

"We're probably thinking of the scene where Lokki gave his jacket to Cosi."

"Yes, but I didn't do it purposely," I rectified.

"I believe you. And look, I now have my own leather jacket," she said a content smile on her face.

Talking about it reminded me of something else that had happened in that very scene. They held hands while walking to the ballroom we were making our way too. It was the only thing not happening. Sometimes the past is best forgotten. I've gotten to be paranoid. If the past was to happen again, in the same way, we all know how it'll end. And because of that hard-to-believe stupid reason, I didn't hold her hand. Something else was different. The use of a GPS. Though if they had it, they would have used it. The evolution of technology probably wasn't relevant in this odd situation.

"I'm wondering," she began, snapping me out of my over-thinking mind. "What exactly do we do once we get there? We can't really say: Excuse me, but do you perhaps still have the leather jacket of a certain man called Lokki? He came here about 80 years ago." She threw her arms in the air. "What kind of look would we get?" she said, making me laugh uncontrollably. We both had this in common, going into things with little thinking.

"You're definitely right, but I say it's worth a try, and if it doesn't work out, we'll get a big laugh out of it for years to come."

"True. But let's not forget other possibilities. Maybe the jacket became a monument."

"A monument?" I gave her the look we would probably receive at the party venue if we spouted our nonsense.

"Think about it. They found a dead man on the grass behind their ballroom and maybe the guy who arranged the coats said: Hey! I remember this man, he's the one who wore a leather jacket to a high-class event. And since it was a tragedy, they kept the jacket to remember him."

"Or they sent it to a family member." I was

able to cut her story short with a single phrase. The glow in her eyes dimmed, and I felt bad seeing it. "I'm sorry."

"No, no, you may be right, but if you are, we have more work to do. There will be a long trail to follow. Finding a family member and-"

"I think that's what we should have done first," I remarked, realizing that we were idiots.

She face palmed herself and, "There was an easier road and we," she couldn't finish her sentence. I didn't blame her.

"But we're..." I peeped at the screen on her phone, "two minutes away from our destination. It would be a shame."

"Let's follow our destiny then," she said, not realizing how scary that statement had sounded to me.

Chapter 16

Sol's point of view

Destiny, you say. A big sense of realization came to me. It rushed its way to my head, giving me whiplash. The enjoyable, heartwarming walk filled with butterflies suddenly gave me goosebumps. It felt so wrong to walk on a road you were supposed to walk on. It was all predetermined. I lost all words.

"What changed?" I asked him without context.

"What changed?" he said back, and I had to

face palm myself again. What was wrong with me that day, the feeling of being a puppet really sank in and made me an empty wooden doll.

"This déjà vu might just be an actual déjà vu and our meeting? I may not have noticed you because you sang at the Cherry and I was not writing a novel but we still first met at the same spot and ended up going to the same location. I'm scared because I know what happened behind the ballroom," I explained, speaking in a speedy manner. I was losing my breath, speaking too fast, waving my hands. In other words, I panicked.

"Something did change," Eugene said, laying his hands on my shoulders reliving all of my tense muscles. "We're conscious of it. They weren't. They didn't have a manuscript, we do. If the past is repeating itself, we can prevent it." Thankfully, someone still had a brain. Though his words were of immense comfort, my mind couldn't help but endlessly going towards a single thought.

"I understand, and maybe we shouldn't go to this place. By comforting me, you also brought a reason as to why we shouldn't do the same. You know, we have the chance to change directions," I said, hoping he'd change his mind because my mind goes blank when thinking of what could happen when we open those doors we were so close to.

"You have a point, but..." He wasn't convinced and I don't blame him. A part of me also felt that another chance stood in that room. We could change directions inside the ballroom and who knows if this even is the location we were looking for. Maybe they destroyed the ballroom and built a fast food there and this venue we found is just another one that happened to be there.

I held his hand before he could finish his sentence—my own hand tingling.

"It's alright, I *just* understood your point too. We should go there." His eyes. They got bigger again. Is it because I agreed with him or was he shy I held his hand? If it's the latter, that's pretty cute.

We both took deep breaths before pushing the glass doors open and stepping into what we initially thought would be our worst nightmare. Was it? Will it be?

There was a front desk high enough to think the person behind was standing and not sitting. Approaching we saw she had a chair equally high, good for her. The woman with curly brown hair batted her fake eyelashes while she prepared her smile for us, the customers.

"How may I help you today?"

I looked at Eugene, and he looked at me. Man, that was awkward. We didn't know what to say and *who* should say it. Like everything else we did, we should've thought it through. The woman, impatient, tapped on the counter with her index finger.

"Um," I said, unsure of what comes next.

"This might sound crazy..." Eugene started for me.

"But we were wondering if this place perhaps was a ballroom around 80 years ago, say in the 30s?" I winced, saying the last part.

After the nerve-wracking staring contest I shared with her, she, at last, came up with an answer, "Yes, and?"

"She said yes!" I exclaimed to Eugene, and without context, people would have thought I'd just proposed. We high-fived and he took the relay.

"Again, we were wondering if you possibly have a leather jacket that a man named Lokki left here, 80 years ago," he said, his voice getter quieter by the word. I'm sure the whole time he spoke, he was praying for the jacket to, in fact, be a monument.

Sadly, we received the exact look we expected, raised eyebrows, hands on hip, head leaning down, showing a double chin.

I took the relay, "I told you it'll sound crazy, but if there's any way you could get this type of information, it would be highly appreciated. You see, this man died, and that's the last thing there is left to him," I told her, sounding more desperate and saddened than earlier. These emotions weren't completely fake. I simply exaggerated them. I could see in the corner of my eyes that Eugene was... Impressed. Our dark humour knew no end.

Hearing my desperate plea, her attitude towards us changed. She took off the hand that rested on her hip, eyebrows were lowered, no more double chin on the radar, and she took out a humongous book from the mysterious cabinets behind the counter. The cover was leathery black and the word "guest" was engraved on it in gold. Pages stuck out and most were yellow, presumably because of old age. These papers must have been as old as the people mentioned in it.

"This is an ancient book. We supposedly should keep it in a glass box to protect it, but there wasn't any space anymore."

"There's a monument alright," Eugene discreetly whispered to me, making it so hard to keep my widow-style expression on.

"Your guy's name's probably in there and on his line you'll see if they returned the coat to its owner and if not, what they did with it will be mentioned. That's all I can do but look fast because if my boss caught you, we're all done for." She sounded so nice, but in that last part, I was reminded of my strict mother, though I understood her perspective. We thanked her. I even shook her hands, showing her I was extremely grateful for the nice deed.

We sat on a money-green sofa—designed for the people who waited for a consultant to organize the perfect event—and opened the book that looked to be twice the size of a bible.

"This place was very popular," I remarked.

"This is no times for jokes, we have to be serious." I deserved to be mocked with the same words I used on him at the Cherry.

"I know, I know, but really, even if we had unlimited time, we'd need to spend nights on this. It's not like we can split the work, that'd be destroying their monument."

"You know, we had a lot of *something* these days," he said.

"Something? Elaborate, please."

"We have luck. Why don't we just open the book on a random page?" Just how many times did I need to face palm? This one was different because my hand reached my forehead not on account of my stupidity but *his*. Without having the chance to reply, he took the book and opened it at a random page. I sat there looking at him, scrutinizing his lucky page.

"No luck?" I asked him, knowing the answer. His pouting lips gave it away. "Why don't we be strategic with it? Let's search for the days after the date we saw on the manuscript?" Now who had the brains?

"You're a genius!" he almost shouted, quieting down in the middle.

"I know, I know, now flip to the 30s." My words were thy command.

We searched through it all quite fast. I was afraid we'd be too fast and miss his name. Thankfully, the luck that Eugene talked of did come to us. Lokki Cross, it read. Lokki wasn't and still isn't a common name, thus there were no doubts it was him. And as expected, the "not picked up" case was crossed.

"Let's see what happened to it," he muttered under his breath, following the line with his finger. My eyes also followed his finger until it rested on the answer we'd been looking for.

"Returned to family," I read, only to let out a sigh.

"At least we have confirmation of our next step." Eugene tried to bring out some kind of positivity. Unlike me, he was the type to see the light hidden in the shadows. I envied him once again.

"I'm so tired," I said, feeling all my thoughts curling into a knot.

"The rest is gonna be easy. Don't worry, we have something called the Internet now." His face was so comic I couldn't help but give in and smile. How could I have resisted the shoulders up and the sly smile leaning to the right? A quick pat on the shoulder and I regained the force to stand up again.

"I'll go return the book and we can go."

The nice lady waited for us rather impatiently. She bit her nails, moved her eyes restlessly, and nervously tapped the keys of her keyboard. I suppose that me walking towards her with the holy grail lifted a weight off her shoulders. She clasped her hands together and was almost ready to hug me.

"Oh! You're done! Thank you for bringing it so fast. I hope you found what you were looking for." her voice had sounded airy and much different from earlier. I had seen three distinct faces from a single person.

"Yes, thank you. We found what we were looking for. It's been a tremendous help."

"Oh, I'm glad." Now, she felt like the rich lady in the neighbourhood that calls everyone *darling*. "Oh, how are you today, *darling?*" "Oh, I haven't seen you in a while, *darling*."

We were out of the ballroom when Eugene had yet another one of his realization.

"See, things are already different. We didn't dance in the ballroom, now did we?" I remarked.

"Yes, we dogged a bullet," I replied, looking down at my feet.

I was glad we deviated from the rails that would bring us to our doom. It's great, it is. Somehow, sharing a dance in an empty ballroom under a magnificent chandelier sounded great too. I don't know if at that moment it was the puppeteer speaking or if it was a little girl's spirit still in my heart—the one who'd watched Romeo and Juliet dancing in a ballroom and dreamed of it ever since. Deep down, I knew I wanted to sway with no other but him. In a way, in a tragically beautiful way, Lokki and Cosi had shared their last dance together, just like the love birds everyone knew of.

Life had gotten confusing, and everything was spinning. I also may have started to fall in love.

Eugene's point of view

Back at the Cherry, we were typing away. Rectification, she was typing away. I... caught myself staring at the freckles underneath her eyes. Sol had tiny and barely noticeable freckles, and you really had to stare deeply in order to notice them. She was so focused on the screen that she didn't notice me gawking. Hell, I didn't notice I was gawking myself. Once I did, nothing changed except for the fact I was purposely gawking. Every time, I saw her under a new light and there are no words to describe how I saw her. Words were too superficial in this case. This newly found obsession was a complete mystery to me. Was I following a predestined path? Is there a reason for that path? Or was I following my beating heart?

"Did you find anything?" she said, not looking, making that beating heart jump.

"No, not yet," I quickly said, scrambling to open a window on my laptop. In the process of that, I almost fell as my chair wobbled. Strange, don't you think? It was fine around thirty minutes ago and my seat wasn't warm when I sat back on it. I slowly turned to the counter, glaring at a snickering Bruno.

"Are you okay?" she asked, and I dropped my glare at the speed of lightning.

"I'm fine. It's just the chair." I wriggled in it, showing the wobbliness of it.

"Oh, you should switch with another one or I could go ask Bruno."

"It's fine. A wobbling chair never killed anyone," I replied, hoping this so-called joke would switch the subject.

"If you say so."

"Did you find anything?" I asked at my turn.

A smile appeared on her heart-shaped

face. "I found a news article about the band playing here and an obituary."

"You found an obituary?"

"Yes, with that I found the location of his grave and what the only family member he had left said about him."

"What does it say? Do we have a name?"

"There's no name." Sol sighed before reading the obituary. "Lokki was an average man. He enjoyed playing music in his free time and wasting paper on something he called lyrics. I am saddened by his death." Her mouth set in a grim line, "Well, I might be wrong, but I don't think his family cherished him."

I scoffed. "Makes me feel lucky about having a family that loves me."

"Not everyone has that. I feel grateful too."

"You know, I think we, once again, took a step not noticing the short cut under our nose."

"What short cut?" she crossed her arms.

"We now know where he was buried, but we could have known that without having to research. He passed away near here and I don't think there's gonna be a million of cemeteries near here..." Sol tried hard to not raise her hand again and press it against her forehead. She tightly held on the end of her shirt.

"And you know what else we could've thought of?"

"Hit me."

"Cosi also died near and her grave could be in the same cemetery." My mind was blown. It was small details like that who made me doubt of my brain. I never thought I was smart or anything, but... I was disappointed with myself.

"What's wrong with us?" I told her.

"We're just slow, today. It can happen."

"Twice in a row?"

"Third times the charm." Even she knew how nonsensical it sounded.

"I don't think this saying goes with our situation."

"I know, but I couldn't miss the opportunity." Again, we ended our conversation with smiles and laughs. We left the coffee shop and made our way to our next destination. I was living in an adventure movie. Even though I was a photographer, nothing wild happened to me in my day-to-day life and I can now say that I am living.

"You know, I think we're spending too

much money on coffee in a single day. How many times will we go back to the Cherry today?" she said.

"It's our secret base," I answered, feeling quirky.

"I always wanted to have a secret base." her eyes lit up with excitement. The child inside her was speaking, "as an only child, I always dreamed of making camp in the living room with pillows and blankets. I tried it once, but it was lonely, fell apart quickly and my mom scold me for it."

"I did it a couple of time too with my older brother. We brought it to the next level by camping in the wilderness. There's a gap age between us and my parents trusted him enough to bring me along his trips."

"That must've been fun. I'm getting a little jealous."

"We could go camping together someday," I suggested.

"You mean it?"

"I don't throw empty words," I answered, curving my lips.

"I could just hug you," she said, skipping away.

If she could, why didn't she?

"It's gonna be something," Sol continued, "Seeing their graves and…" she didn't finish her sentence and neither could I. It could be emotional. There's nothing we couldn't expect anymore. Our souls might feel a type of sadness when being reunited with Lokki and Cosi.

"What do you think will happen to us there?"

"I'm not sure what we'll even be doing there? This is another step of ours that feels carved."

"Some things maybe are meant to follow and they'll not necessarily lead us to a tragedy, right?"

"Well, we are walking to our graves right now. What could that mean?" she said, her voice full of sarcasm.

"The saying you tried to use earlier fits this realization I just had," I said.

"All we do is realize today." Her arms were thrown the air as she shook her head.

"Maybe the third time is the charm."

"I think I understand where you're going because I just had the same realization."

"And that's what we call telepathy. Lokki

and Cosi dreamt of each other and the dreams eventually became reality." I turned to pass her the mic.

"That story and their soul connection could mean there were others before them."

"And in this order, we would be…"

At the same time, we said: "the third life!" we used the exact same words.

"Maybe they failed the two other times and this time…"

"I think we deserve our happy ending," I said so suddenly. "I mean, we learned from their experience and that could save our lives this time," I rectified, my eyes shifting nervously.

A sly like smirk of a smile formed on Sol's face. She said nothing, but I knew what kind of words awaited me. She opened her mouth to speak, but soon closed it. To my vast surprise, she just let it go and walked on—the grin wasn't erased. I was too embarrassed to ask for an explanation and only followed her.

An awkward silence filled the road. Even the crunching sound of fallen leaves sounded quiet to me. I had created this mess and now I had to sort it out, but the coming words seemed like a continuation of the rectification.

"We should recapitulate what we've learned from them and make a list of things best to avoid if we don't want to end up laying next to them."

I pretended to only care about protecting our lives rather than making this connection work in case we weren't on the same page and I'd made a fool of myself. We did only meet a while ago, in the material world.

"One thing we could do is stay away from Kylo if we knew who he was," she said, making a good point.

"I have an inkling of an idea of who it could be, so hear me out."

"I'm always listening."

"Bruno," I threw out.

"It's far-fetched, but could be. What are the odds?"

"Huh," I scoffed, "What are the odds of meeting in a place where two people who look exactly like us first met too?"

"Okay, you have a point."

"I have another theory. Kylo wore plaid every day and Bruno wears Hawaiian shirts every day."

"That's even more far-fetched, but seeing what happened to us, it's possible."

"If we had a picture of this Kylo, we could confirm it. For now, I don't want you near Bruno."

"How? what?" She looked at me, mouth wide open.

"I'm dead serious. We're learning from their missteps, and I don't want to scare you, but if we keep changing things, it's not guaranteed to end well. You've heard of the butterfly effect where one slight change messed up everything. It's your life that could be in danger more than me." I caught my breath for a second before getting back to it. "If there's even a slight possibility that Kylo was the killer and that he is Bruno in this life, well, you shouldn't be with him."

"Wait, yes, my life could be in danger because of this butterfly effect, but Kylo had a motive. Bruno wouldn't kill me. We shouldn't forget rationality."

"I'm just worried," is all I said, holding her arm. "Even if you don't see a reason for it, do it for me." I had made a reason, and I wished she would accept it. I knew very well that this was stupid, that I was being paranoid and that perhaps my jealousy might have taken a part in it, but it felt right that way.

"Alright, I'll try. It's not like I even want to be near him. I have to for my daily dose of caffeine," Sol had answered nonchalantly.

"I'll be the one to take your order, now."

"You do what you want."

"Oh, I will," I said, surprising myself.

In just a couple of steps, we'll be right in front of the late Cosima and Lokki. My heart wavered and my hands shook from the uneasiness rising in me. It was hard to handle, but I wasn't alone. I had next to me someone precious. Someone strong.

Chapter 18

Sol's point of view.

I'd never been to a cemetery in the past. How strange is it that the first time I come here is to see perhaps my old body buried? If the two are in fact us, then this body we have is yet another vessel. And the bodies laying underground might be soulless. I wonder what the souls who lead us here would feel reuniting with their old vessel. Will there be a reaction? Will the earth stop orbiting for a millisecond? Will the moon flicker? Will stars fall down the sky? I don't think it's a normal thing to happen and my pessimist mind only goes to the worst-case scenarios such as the idea that it may not be a good idea. It doesn't seem natural. Won't there be consequences? As much as I wanted to share my insane worries with Eugene, I'd feel bad. We already decided to go and we're going and oh my, we're here, in front of the Victorian style black metal gate. Behind the gate, you could see nothing but smog. Scary movies seem a bit too realistic to me now. In fear, I unconsciously walked behind Eugene. I almost grabbed the edge of his hoodie, but I kept myself under control.

"We're here!" Unlike me, he had a smile on his face. Oh, How the tables have turned.

"Yes, we are." My voice was soulless. "Don't you think it's a little eerie?" I said, hinting that there was something to fear.

"I think it looks cool," he said, unaware of my fright. Where did our telepathy go? Wasn't he supposed to know how I felt? Maybe if he looked into my eyes. I tugged on his hoodie to get his attention. It worked. He looked back at me with a questioning look on his face. I said nothing and let him watch. He looked confused, and I noticed his pupils had a bit of an edge on the bottom making them resemble diamonds and they were so black, it felt like looking right into a black hole. I didn't focus so much on showing him I was scared anymore and thus, I failed.

"It's nothing. Let's go in." With heavy steps, I let him push the gates open, and we entered. Chills and an icy wind passed through me. The cemetery was so much more obscure from the inside. The grass was like quicksand and I walked in it, knowingly, with the impression that the gate would shut by itself, trapping us in.

On the right and the left side, there were graves, multiple ones. Some were clean and looked taken care of, while dirt and moss covered some, making the written names illegible. They had been forgotten and disregarded. I found myself looking at those more, fearing they'd be the ones we were looking for.

"Do you think their graves are next to each other?" Eugene asked me, hands in the middle pocket of the hoodie I returned earlier in the coffee shop.

"I'm not so sure. Nobody really knew about their relationship or the fact they knew each other except maybe for Kylo, but he certainly wouldn't have buried them next to each."

"You have a point," he sighed. "I hope you're wrong, though." I wasn't offended and hoped he was right.

"Do you think we could bring them together if they're not already?"

"Sure, we just need to displace a couple of dead people, no biggie. Let's ask at the front desk." His joke lightened everything and drove away some of the fear I felt. I was glad to be by his side, but I wanted more.

"Listen, I have a weird request."

"I'm listening."

"Would it be okay if we held hands while walking? I'm a little scared to be in a cemetery and…" I didn't get to finish explaining when he grabbed my hand, without a word or a change of expression, just a poker face. And here came the butterflies, again—they've never left, actually.

We didn't say a thing after and just walked. I honestly could have missed the names we were looking for, even if they were right under my nose. It's just that his hand is so warm and mine was freezing cold. I felt heat rising to my cheeks. They probably were red like cherry tomatoes, and the cold that surrounded us wasn't enough to calm them down.

"Try not to look at the graves. Maybe close your eyes," he suddenly spoke.

"How will I read the names?"

"I'll do that. Just stay close." Eugene pulled me closer and did the unthinkable—well, at least for me—he intertwined our fingers, tightening his grip. That's it. My heart hit the stop sign. Damn you butterflies, why are you flapping your wings so much? I'm dying out here.

"Sol," he called out. We didn't say each other's names often, so it always gave me shivers. "I think I found Lokki." I quickly faced the direction his eyes went to and indeed there was a grave with the name *Lokki Cross* written on it. Seeing it brought out feelings that had been locked inside of me. Before I knew it, my eyes welled up and silent tears rolled down the cheeks that froze once more.

"I- I don't know what's happening to me," I said, my voice breaking. Eugene, who looked concerned, took me in. He brought his arm around me and my head perfectly laid under his neck, on his chest.

"You don't need to know or understand,"

he said in a much lower voice. "Let it out," he continued while I now properly wept, gasping for air. If Cosi was in me, then it is natural to feel sadness ripping your heart apart when hit by the sight of your lover's grave. It still was fascinating when my lover was the one patting my back, aiding me to let go of the pain. The dead man was here with me. It could be a sad picture if he was a ghost but, Eugene is a living human. Thinking this way relieved a part of my sadness and the tears were slowly reduced. I could not thank him enough for being patient and helping me through the abrupt breakdown I was having.

"I just can't help it," I tried to say without letting out gasps in between words.

"You don't need to justify anything, even if others think you're a lunatic. Know that I understand you." Yes, he may be the only one on this earth or universe who understands me because we're in it together.

"Another thing that makes me sad is that death was really the end for them. If they reincarnated in us, they merged and lost themselves. Cosi and Lokki aren't watching us from the sky or something like that. They are us. We consumed them." I cracked. Rather than tears, I was afraid, and I froze.

"I wouldn't say we consumed them, neither are they lost. If they are in us, we are them. How do I explain that?" Eugene was as lost as I was. It wasn't a simple thing to explain. I couldn't. "We are Lokki and Cosi," he continued as I looked up to his face, "we just don't remember. Now that's clearer isn't it?"

"Yes, it is. If we fully believe, if we take this fact in, we are Cosi and Lokki." I had a breakthrough and was transported through different dimensions. It took only a glance at Eugene, and I legitimately did the unthinkable myself. With both hands, I held his cheeks, stood on my tippy toes, leaned in, and pressed my lips against his. His shoulders tensed up but were quickly brought down when he held my waist. Absolute bliss is how I can describe this kiss. His lips, it was like kissing a soft peach. What was a soft peck soon become a seesaw-like kiss, passionate and, in this case, emotional. Memories were artificial, but this feeling was real. It was not something you could cultivate in a few days. I could never meet someone else and have this burning flame I have with Eugene.

I pulled out, merely a few centimetres

away.

"There were never four or six people. It was always us," I said, my breath merging with his. I didn't have to doubt my love for him. We were just wasting time falling all over again. Deep down, we knew of our feelings but suppressed them in case of embarrassment. It seemed too fast. However, realizing that our love was much deeper and much older broke the barriers. Who knows, we might have loved each other for centuries but always missed each other because when we learned the truth, it was already too late.

Eugene gave the smile that melted me each time. It was such a familiar one. I felt a magic twinkle every time his lips slightly curved and his eyes sparkled. I knew I'd seen it somewhere.

"It will always be us," he said, leaning in to be the one planting his lips this time.

Cosmic feelings I had said they were in a past life. Well, I was right, completely. Only, I did not have the flashes mentioned in the manuscript. I took it as a good sign that no picture of tears flew through my mind. We were going to make it. Being closer than ever, lips on lips, with only good thoughts.

Eugene's point of view

The one who had the flashes was me. I saw the tears; I saw the pain and was horrified. The threat hadn't passed; it remained close. More than ever, it roamed and being conscious of it was terrifying. It was a pain and a fear to be kept to oneself. Cosi had done the same. Sure, it didn't end well, but I know much more now. There was one solution I had thought of in order to keep her safe. From all that occurred, I could tell that harm was coming for Sol. My harm would be seeing *her* harmed.

I took both of her hands and looked her straight in the eyes.

"Would you like to go away somewhere, for a couple of days, with me? We could be at peace and forget about it all for a while." Figured I could keep her safe if she was by my side each and every hour of the day until the threat passed. Being away from Mardi Town could help as well. We would be outside of the stage where the play happens.

"And where would we go?"

"Earlier, I spoke about my camping trips with my older brother. I could take you on one. Trust me, I have a lot of experience."

"Oh, I trust you, but really?" Her eyes flickered with joy. "I would love to! It has always been a dream of mine." Her knees bent and her feet tried their best to stay put on the gravel in order to not jump around.

"It's decided then. What do you think of the beach for a camping spot?" With that, she gasped.

Knees straitening up, she spoke: "I- I need to tell you something." Now I was nervous. "When I told you about the dreams I had, I didn't go into much detail, but there is one particular dream where we both were at the beach at night."

"Did it feel ominous?"

"No, it was good. It felt pleasant. You showed me a fascinating rainbow."

"At night?"

"It's weird, right?"

"Not at all," I reassured her. "We must have seen a moonbow."

"A moonbow?"

"A moonbow is a rainbow you can see at night and it's pretty rare."

"That could be a good sign, no?"

"Oh, definitely," no lie came out of my mouth. Rainbows meant happiness, and something as precious as a moonbow would simply mean rare happiness, such as a one of a kind connection. Yet another confirmation came, making the remaining doubts fly away like little butterflies.

"I hope we'll get to see this moonbow," she told me and I fell deeper.

"It's my dream to photograph one, actually. Tell me, in your dream, did I have a camera hanging down my neck?"

"I couldn't see your face very well and you want me to remember a detail like that?"

"Got it. I will bring my camera on the trip."

"I can't wait."

The staring contests we had were quite special. It's strange how either of us found it hard to look away. I usually wouldn't have the courage to look into someone's eye for more than a few seconds. I would be nervous by the third second. With Sol, it was the exact contrary. By the third second, my eyes were locked, and it takes a while to unlock them. Honestly, who wouldn't fall into these moss-green eyes? Bring me that person, if they exist. On second thoughts, don't bring them.

"If you are ready, maybe we could peek at Lokki's grave now," I asked her, careful to not force her into something that showed itself to be heartbreaking. We'd been near the grave, but I showed my back to it, covering Sol's sight of it. I wondered if painful feelings would stir in me as well when encountering Cosi's grave. Lokki hadn't seen a dead Cosi since he passed on first.

"I am ready. Why wouldn't I when Lokki is right next to me, holding my hand?" I scoffed, not in a negative tone, in one that meant to say, *that's funny.*

The grave was squeaky clean, the engraved

name looked perfectly clear. And freshly picked sunflowers stood on top, making me think it was well taken care of. The family member who seemed to not love him much took care of the grave, or maybe it could have been a close friend of his.

"What do we do in front of a grave?" she asked me.

"I'm fortunate enough to never have had to be in front of a grave, so my guess is as good as yours."

"Maybe show our respects?"

"Sure, we could also just say a little something to him."

Sol looked down at the grave, her free hand coming to her stomach, politely: "I'll start. Hello, Mr. Lokki, you might have been the same age as us when you were alive, but now you'd be old, really old. I don't know if you'd even be alive?"

"You're making the man roll in his grave." I got hit in the arm for that comment.

She continued, "I would have loved to listen to you play some music. I envy Cosi for having heard you. You see, in this life, I have no recollection of it." Her message tickled my brain. "I'm sorry you died the way you died and perhaps we'll find the person responsible and…"

"Don't finish that sentence. I know what you're going to say and it's not legal."

"What if I really wanted to avenge his death" she said, her polite hand turning into a fist.

"You know what they say, don't do the crime if you can't do the time. Wouldn't you rather spend that time with me?"

She sighed, "You're right, why are you repeatedly right?"

"It's my gift."

Sol, I think enjoyed to hit me in the arm. Most of the time, I deserved it.

"Mr. Lokki, or just Lokki, be well. If you are inside Eugene right now, then…" She turned to face me, "Hello."

A new smile was shown, a bit mischievous and pretty. Her cheekbones reached the eyes and her lips were amused.

"I love you," I said without having an internal huddle prior to blurting out such strong words.

"Whoa, whoa, when we say hello, we'd expect: Hi, nice to meet you. You, mister, know no limits. But if you are going to greet me this way, it would only be fair to do the same." Glancing away from me, as if she was shy, she told me, "I love you too."

Now it was my turn to speak with Lokki. As strange as it was, I did. I say strange since, technically, I'd always be speaking to him in my mind.

"Lokki, my friend." Sol chuckled, hearing these words that sounded somewhat awkward. She apologized, and I was back on track. "I promise to you I will care for your Cosi and my Sol. I will make sure we live happily ever after."

"Do you think true love exists?" Sol said, out of nowhere. "Do you believe in the happily ever after story? I'm confused because in the past they told us to believe in it and now they tell us it's all fake."

"It's hard to comprehend, I know. Rather than believing in the happily ever after, we should believe in ourselves and in our connection." I told her, rubbing the cold out of her red hands.

"You're full of wisdom. At this age, it's impressive."

"At this age? We're not that far apart. We only have a two-year gap."

I understood her feelings and the incertitude behind them. How could we believe in love when we didn't understand it? How could we when divorces were so common? Many married only to get divorced in the first couple of years or the ones after. It was rare and amazing to see elderly couples celebrating their 50th or 60th anniversary while still being full of love. Who knows which side we would be on at the end of our journey in this life?

"I guess we should go see Cosi now." She took one last glance at the grave. "Goodbye Lokki, I'll come again, someday."

I bid my farewells in my mind, knowing he'll be able to hear them.

"Do you think someone took care of Cosi's grave just as well as Lokki's? Reading her manuscript, I think she lived alone and for a long time," Sol remarked.

"We'll never really know the back story."

"It's a shame we won't."

As we wandered around the empty cemetery filled with smog, something struck.

"Do you think it would be weird if I

whipped out my camera and took pictures of the graves?"

"Which ones?"

"Lokki's and Cosi's, maybe also the graves with names not visible..." I feared her reaction.

"It would have meaning so... Not so weird." With the confirmation of my soulmate, I took out my film camera. It fit the mood more than a professional and modern camera.

"You won't be able to check the photos until you develop them."

"It is a dilemma, but with time, you learn to take brilliant pictures prior to seeing them alive."

"Your passion shows in your words," she told me, warming my heart. The only acknowledgment that mattered now was hers and mine.

My eye was in the viewfinder, my knee on the floor, and I was almost ready to hit the shutter. As Sol remarked it, I wouldn't have the chance to look at the picture right away. Thus, I took my time and stayed there until my knee hurt from being pressed too long against the hard gravel. This act continued on for a couple more pictures of unnamed graves. There was something aesthetic about them. Photographs sometimes gave out emotions and I already feel that these will give out sorrow and a sense of abandonment. I tried my best to properly convey what they were, though something troubled my head.

"I'm sorry," I said to Sol, lowering my camera and standing up, my knee sore and most probably marked with the shape of the floor.

"Why would you be sorry?"

"It must be boring having to wait for me."

"Nonsense," she replied, her face softening. "It's one thing you love and seeing you so invested only makes me happy. I'll tell you what, I'll go look for Cosi's grave and speak to her first and you can comfortably click that shutter as much as you want. We could even stay till tomorrow, I don't mind," she said, patting my head like it was a loaf of bread. Then she pranced away on her black loafers. So that's what it feels like to have won the lottery.

Sol's point of view

I roamed the cemetery all by myself, looking for my previous vessel. The fear of not being able to find it grew by the minute. Would we have to rub the moss out of every grave to find her? Would she even be here? What if nobody found out she died until years after or a million eviction notices and they cremated her to save space? I over thought and brought in negativity to my head. Thinking "What would Eugene say?" helped me clear it away. He was much more of a positive person than I was and always found the right words to make the bruise all better. Continuing on that path, I thought: "Let's have faith we will find her name and if her name is covered, why not just wipe the moss away?"

The smog wasn't really helping, why even was the smog only present here? It was a sunny day and I can assure you that outside the cemetery, it still was a sunny day. This place crept me out, but... Eugene was near and so I felt fine. There's nothing to add to this statement. It's pretty self-explanatory. Oh, he looked so cute with his small film camera that was entirely covered by his hands. It wasn't a fancy one. I remember them from my childhood. It was the small disposable one that came in either yellow or green. They were next to the cash register in every corner shop. Oddly, I remembered he had another film camera much more sophisticated than this one. I wonder why he used another?

I multi-tasked glancing at Lokki doing bizarre poses to click the perfect pictures and read out the names on the graves I passed. Never in my life did I think I'd use these words in the same sentence, nor did I think I'd learn to be productive in a cemetery. Multi-tasking was a first for me.

Walking with dropped shoulders, I grew anxious and once again negative. The positivity I'd held on to for some time flew away. It was gone with the wind. A previous research taught me that the name Cosima was old and at the time might have been common. It seemed to have been the case anywhere other than Mardi Town, as I had not seen a single grave with her name. Perhaps this was a good thing, it not being common here. Without the knowledge of her last name, it'd be impossible to know which grave belonged to the Cosi we'd been looking for.

Having looked through all the named graves, I knew it was time to get my hands dirty and look through the unnamed ones. Just as we did for the guest book, we'd need to be smart about this. There were hundreds of unnamed graves and in this cold, I'd freeze to death wiping the dirt away from each one. Now believing in the concept of spirituality, I closed my eyes and sat on the floor—not caring that my pants would drown in dust—to somehow meditate. Perhaps my soul will feel called to its old vessel. I'd feel a tug and see a red cross on the treasure map. I didn't know if it would work that way. I just imagined it would. I wasn't much a spiritual guru, nor did I read enough about it. The fact that it felt right was the spiritual part of it.

My eyes itched to open to check on Eugene, and my lips itched to open to explain to him what I was doing so he wouldn't make fun of me. Realizing his silly stretches could also be made fun of left me feeling better about myself. If he ever dared to laugh at me, I could tell him: "What about you?"

Taking deep breaths—I heard were important to take from yoga videos—I started to meditate. Darkness was the only thing surrounding me. No treasure map or tugging had come. I figured it could take some time, and I had time. Or did I?

I had lost myself in this world I created from silence and emptiness. I tried to listen to words that only the heart could hear. I tried to feel a force pushing me towards a light that could only be seen when it was pitch black, like a star in the night sky. My mind was skeptical, but perhaps not enough because I felt my heart wavering or just beating irregularly in a way to give out a message. How could I decipher the words of a beating heart? I didn't have to. Once again, it all just felt right. My eyes still closed, I stood and paced around, following the beat. I matched my steps with the sound of it and indeed; it lead me somewhere.

"This is it," I said to myself, breaking the silence. Not only did I break the silence, but the entire world created by my soul. My eyes snapped open and there I was, standing in front of a grave covered with moss and dirt—more than the others. Without hesitation, I approached it, sat on my knees, and wiped away with bare fingers. The rock it was made of was freezing, but the rapid movements I executed warmed my hands a tiny bit. It was still painful. The first letters I could see were: D and A. They were on the right, which meant that was the start of a last name. I hadn't lost hope and brushed away continuously until the moss completely entered my fingernails. Soon enough, the full name appeared to be visible.

"Cosima Daine," I read out loud, feeling a weight leaving my shoulders. Relieved, I let my butt hit the grass and struggled to keep tears of joy and exhaustion under. That day had proved itself to be a roller coaster of emotions foreign to me. Normally, tears weren't my forte nor were any sort of emotions unless you'd call being lost an emotion.

Just when I was about to call out for Eugene, he appeared behind me, giving me the biggest fright.

"You scared me!"

"I'm sorry. I ran here because you were suspicious."

"Suspicious?"

"Here, I'll help you." he gave me a hand to stand up, and I reluctantly took it—my hands were very dirty. "You were walking with closed eyes and scratched away with fury." While he laughed I thought of taking out my *how about you?* line, but other things seemed more important.

"I found Cosi's grave."

"I can see. It must've been tough since the name was covered. How did you find it so quickly?"

"It's a long story, one I'll tell you about later."

"Alright then, let's speak to Cosi first."

I caught my breath, "Yes."

"Your nose is red like Rudolf's," he said, pointing at it with a grin.

"Is that so important right now" My cheeks were getting red for a whole different reason than the cold. I felt fumes.

"It is important," he then said, dropping the grin. "You're freezing." Eugene took off his hoodie for the second time that day. I started to think he liked to do that. I questioned his past life. Was he just a singer? No side hustles?

In all seriousness, he was sweet enough to put on me his warm hoodie while he would be the one freezing next.

"Put your hands in the pocket."

"My hands are dirty. They can't go in there."

"I care more about your health than a hoodie I have in different shades."

I raised my eyebrow at him, "Different shades? It's black."

"I have different kinds of black hoodies and grey ones that tilt on black by how dark they are." Cute.

I ended up placing my hands in the pocket and was happily surprised by the warmth that filled it. His hands had been there up until a couple of seconds ago. He covered my head with the hood and it was perfection. Now, more than ever, I was ready to speak.

"Hello Cosi," I said, sensing how stiff my tone was. I nodded a couple of times, for no apparent reasons and continued, "thank you for the manuscript. I'll be sure to tell your story one way or another."

An idea had then struck me.

"What if I completed the manuscript?" I told Eugene. "Our story could be the continuation, and I'll fulfil her dream of publishing a book."

"That's what Cosi would want. She didn't destroy the manuscript, probably for you to pick it up and complete it."

He was right. Cosi didn't write "The End" on the last page, leading me to think she'd wanted the story to be completed and shown to the world. I was handed a precious dream. One that's filled with memories, pain, sadness, bliss, euphoria and more. It felt special to have a project of my own. Something to do with my life. It is a first.

"Thank you, Cosi, for leaving me this enormous responsibility. I will make sure to not disappoint you. I'll try to work as hard as you did to produce this book. The last thing I wanted to say to you is that I'll cherish Lokki and care for Eugene."

Stepping back, I let Eugene have his turn. He seemed nervous, or was it the cold that got to him? Either way, I felt bad. Seeing him shiver, I couldn't help but take him in my arms. Rubbing his arms to warm them up while I listened to his message.

"Dear Cosi, I believe that right now you are in front of me, taking the role of a fireplace." I didn't look up even when he made these types of comments. "I also believe that you are the prettiest person I've ever met and trust me, with my family travelling a lot, I've seen quite the number of people." Instead of hitting his arm like I always did, I rubbed a little harder. Wincing, he continued: "But when I say prettiest, I also meant it heart-wise. Though our memories aren't present in my brain, I'll build new ones. They'll be as good or even better. Thank you for leaving us the manuscript that became the glue to stick us together. Our doubts towards love would have taken us in a whole other direction if it wasn't for the eye-opener."

His arms escaped my grip, and his hands were on my cheeks. His eyes had drooped down and lines formed on his forehead.

"What's wrong?"

"Do you realize we almost never happened? If it wasn't for Cosi, we'd be paralyzed by fear, thinking the other didn't like us. We'd have missed each other and not speak at all."

Feeling his thoughts stream across his eyes, I understood he needed a tight hug. I trapped him and almost killed him by taking away all the oxygen. We connected, and I felt in him something much deeper: a sense of loneliness. This embrace was the comfort he longed for.

"Know, Eugene, that I will always be with you. You only have to call and I'll make you fly."

Chapter 21

Eugene's point of view

We had visited the graveyard, seen both their graves but did not find out anything about the jacket. Okay, maybe we forgot. With all the tears and moving messages, it slipped our mind. It's not like the jacket would be sitting on his grave, anyway. Pure curiosity brought us down there. And the night brought us back home.

On the day I spend alone without Sol, I made it my personal mission to dig more on what happened the night everything ended. In order to protect Sol and prevent anything from happening again, I would need more information. The past wasn't meant to be repeated. My only clue was Bruno, who was most likely to be Kylo. I sensed it through the blood that flowed in my veins. The moment I laid eyes on him, I think I knew this guy was bad news. Right before we parted, the other day, I told Sol not to go to the Cherry. I asked of her to spend the day somewhere else while she works on her novel. In a safer place, preferably her home. That would give me time to investigate Bruno and keep him away from her. Sol didn't believe in my theory and surely wouldn't support the investigation. I felt bad for lying, but for her safety; I did what I had to do.

Today, again, only winks of sleep were recorded. With so much to think about, my head never stopped. There was a hamster on a diet in it, endlessly running on his wheel.

Out of habit, I directly went to the Cherry. The idea of being discreet had flown away the moment I entered the place and matched eyes with the suspect. The silver bell wasn't of much help either. He frowned, as usual, and avoided my eyes the sooner he could. I, for a fact, could not avoid him. His bright red Hawaiian shirt with neon green flowers stood out. He'd have absolutely no problem being visible in a crowd. He'd be the focus point of every performer.

"Hello, Bruno!"

I gave him a big, friendly smile. Since I could not be discreet, I thought I'd go all out and try to get closer and open up his heart. With time, the proof that indeed he was Kylo would show itself. That was my theory. Though, I doubt he'll innocently let me in his circle. I had to play a certain game of manipulation. It is something I've never used before but surfing the internet all night long was always so helpful for these situations that never used to occur.

Again, only by the sight of me, he grimaced, "What can I get for you?" he said, not even bothering to force a smile.

"What do you recommend, my friend?" I was reluctant to add that last word. It seems my mouth was as well.

With raised eyebrows, he opened his mouth to speak, but closed it soon enough. His features all tensed up. If a stare could kill, it wouldn't be his. That expression to me was comic. He tried to appear strong and intimidating. Sorry, my friend, it is the opposite.

"So?" I reminded him.

"I guess the seven shot espresso is good." He was trying to kill me with a grin and an overpowered coffee.

"You're not very creative," I said under my breath, quietly enough for only me to have heard it. My plan wasn't going along so smoothly. It fell through the water and so came Plan B, the not so likable one. "I'll just stick with a cappuccino."

Why was it so hard to befriend him? It's not like he knew I was in a relationship with Sol. For him, I should just be a guy that spoke to Sol. Was he so possessive of someone that wasn't his? Sol never belonged to anyone. This kind of obsessive love is spine chilling because it never ends well. I could now see how everything would unfold. Bruno's reason to end her would probably be that if he cannot have her, nobody could. Merely the sight of him created anger in me. I took it all out on the edge of my hoodie. I tend to grab the end of my clothing and clench my fist really tight when I have anger that needs to be suppressed. Receiving my coffee; I drank it fast, out of spite. After the burning sip pained the roof of my mouth, I bitterly regretted that choice.

From a table I had sat in, my eyes followed his every move. It wasn't a very smart move of me. A barista makes coffee and Bruno did the same. All day long. Should I follow him when he clocks out? That would make me the creep. Confronting him would be an option, not an easy one. There is nothing I could say that wouldn't provoke him. I wonder if Lokki had ever talked to Kylo. He did sing at the café Kylo worked in. Surely, they shared a couple of words. Kylo might also have been jealous of Lokki's popularity and when he approached the girl he was interested in, that's it. The pipe burst. It made more sense for Kylo's fury to have been accumulated rather than it being a one time burst. Even for the 30s, killing wouldn't be the first idea that comes to mind when someone ticked you off, once. I did not have Lokki's popularity, but I had Sol's heart. A part of it. That perhaps gave me more time because there was one less reason for his anger. Bruno was a ticking bomb, and I had to remove the colourful cables with prudence and logic. If I pulled a cable that I wasn't supposed to, a beast would run wild in the streets. The cables all looked like triggers to me. It was hard to figure out which one to pull first. Every step seemed like a poor decision. My patience ran low and my feet were faster than my thoughts. They led me to the counter, staring at Bruno with no words coming out.

"What's up, buddy?" he said, wiping some glass cups. I froze, but I shouldn't have. I needed to be brave and, in this case, smart.

"What do you usually do after work? I only see you making coffees. It makes me wonder what you're up to in your free time." Nothing better came up in my head. Let's just say I was not a witty person, neither was I a smart one.

"None of your business, buddy." He dropped the cup he was cleaning rather strongly. The sound was deafening. I took out the blue cable first and oh, bad decision. I guess.

"Whoa, whoa," I told him. "What do you have against me?" honesty was another approach.

"A vendetta." He replied, scaring me.

"That's a big word, Bruno. You don't know me well enough for a vendetta."

"Oh, I do." his eyes had doubled in size.

"I'm confused. Do you know something I don't?" I know it sounds stupid because I *knew* more than he thought. This, ladies and gentlemen, is the game of manipulation. Maybe he knows of his past life and if I keep pushing him to speak, he might reveal it. He'll spit out the proof all by himself, like a good boy.

Bruno inhaled deeply from his nose, his eyes shifted around as if he had been got caught. I used the big innocent eyes that for him would not be cute, but despicable. For his own good, he'll have to snap and tell me I did him wrong in the past and the present.

Finally, he spoke. "You're a cousin of mine."

My jaw dropped. I was expecting something. Not that.

"What?" I exclaimed, holding on to the counter for balance.

"A distant cousin." I'm glad he clarified it but the blood! The same blood flowed in us? Unbelievable.

"How do you know that and not me? It doesn't even make sense. I recently moved here and have not heard of family anywhere near."

He threw his neck behind in exhaustion.

"You lived here before."

And that was it! Along with a shocking revelation came what I'd been looking for this whole time.

"You mean the 30s?" I threw this small bomb to accelerate the process.

"You know about the 30s?" The roles had been reversed. I was calm and collected while he held on for dear life.

"Of course, Kylo." I was confident enough to say his name since no doubts clouded me anymore.

He gasped. "Since you know about the past, are you deliberately getting close to Sol to hurt me?"

"Now that's where you're wrong. I-" hesitation briefly took over me, but my stupid heart took control. Never only listen to your heart. "I love Sol." That was yet another trigger. I pulled the cable that had a warning sticker on it.

"No, you don't."

"Yes, I do," I couldn't back down. I've done it. Every time something goes wrong, I feel the train going back on the rails, leading to a tragic crash. Everything happens for a reason, they say. Doing my best to change that wasn't enough. Despair hit me fast enough for my head to go blank.

"It's always been like that. You weren't satisfied with all these girls throwing themselves at you. No, you had to go with the one who was in your cousin's sight. Back then, you knew you had a cousin." Perhaps Bruno was born with Kylo's memories and thinks of them as his own.

"I don't have Lokki's memories," I clarified. "I learned of him through a manuscript written by Cosi. And judging by the contents, Lokki truly loved Cosi. It was never a game for him."

Lokki, yes, was surrounded by many people, but his eyes were on only one. The moss green-eyed girl, Cosi. I doubt he was a player. His memories may not be inside my head, but instincts are something you could not ignore.

"You have her manuscript?" Bruno focused more on that part. I have a feeling that the rest of my words entered an ear and went out the other.

"You will not lay a finger on the manuscript or Sol."

I'm afraid it was the last cable and a threat coming from those so-called instincts.

Sol's point of view

At home, I was. All alone with only the sound of my breath and the ticking clock that drove me crazy. On multiple times, I took it upon myself to remove the batteries. The Victorian clock was just a decor and no one ever used it. Heck, my parents weren't home enough to check it. Each time though, one of them noticed, scold me and put back the bloody batteries. Nowadays, it took them longer to realize it was forever five o'clock at home. It went from a couple of hours to a couple of days. I longed to know how long it'll take this time. Since I would be home all day, better be comfortable.

I made a list of coffee shop elements and tried to recreate them in my home. The first one would be the coffee. My dose of caffeine was usually administrated to me at the Cherry. Today was different, as I had to make my own coffee. It is pretty simple. You'd only have to throw a spoon or two of ground coffee, add water and press on a single button. *Easy peasy, lemon squeezy.*

While waiting for the coffee to drip, I turned on some music. To mimic the coffee shop ambiance, I literally searched *coffee shop ambiance* online and found the perfect sound. When I closed my eyes, I could imagine it all. Behind were the machines dripping espressos. Besides, the group of people endlessly talking. In front, the customer walking in the shop. Something was obviously missing. I was getting used to a certain person's company. We spend entire days together and now it wasn't Sol and Eugene's day but Sol's solo day. It's a shame, really. We only started to be honest with each other yesterday. What can I do? Eugene said he had something important to do. He mentioned we could see each other later in the day when he's done. That alone cheered me up.

Sol's solo day was to be used productively. Ignoring my college work, I was going to focus on the novel. A powerful urge was born in me when this magical idea hit me. I wanted to fulfil Cosi's wish and discover for myself this work I apparently did in a past life. Perhaps typing out a story will ignite a burning fire that was dormant for years. Let's see if that passion remained with time or if I am meant to do something different in this life. Eugene has a different passion. He likes photography while Lokki enjoyed music.

The beeping sound of the coffee machine was the sound I waited for. I ever only drank cold coffee and had to pour an insane amount of ice in my glass. I rued that choice… Hot coffee immediately poured onto ice cubes would melt them, thus adding water and diluting the coffee, making it weaker. There was no way I'd waste freshly made coffee, so I took it to my workspace in the dining room. I made an extra pot of coffee, letting it chill for later. The only thing left to do was work, the dreaded part. It excited me to start something new, despite that, it still was work. One I wasn't used to, nor did I ever try it. A blank page stood on the screen of my laptop. I crossed my hands and laid my head on them, elbows on the table. Cosi's manuscript was complete, but was only a part of the story. I have to complete the entire book by adding the rest. The present portion of it where the main characters succeed to break the curse that chained them to an eternity of tragedy after tragedy. The pressure was real. I not only had to complete the story in writing, but in action as well. I hope to write my own unique ending and not have to copy hers. Okay, that was dark.

Fingers on the keyboard and I typed out our first meeting. Writer's block wasn't quite possible since I was not inventing. I was retelling events. Of course, they are only in my point of view, so not completely accurate. If I get comfortable enough with writing, I could even add insignificant minor details that didn't happen for the fun of it and bring it to the fiction category. Really, there was no need to sprinkle anything on this story. I would be sued if I called this non-fiction because who would believe it? It took me a long time to believe it myself. A third party would think of it as a joke. Laughter slipped its way out. My day was going abnormally well. The coffee was not quite up the mark, but other than that, great. The words smoothly flowed together, creating splendid sentences that I did not know I could create. I was enjoying myself and paid no attention to the watery coffee. Never have I had this much fun while sitting down and doing something you could call work. If I continue to love it this much, it might open new doors. For all one knows, it could.

***

Time flew without notice. The fingers that typed away were stopped by a vibration coming from the phone that rested on my lap. As soon as I perceived Eugene's name on the screen, I lost focus on the novel and my stiff focused face lightened up.

Eugene: Are you home?

Sol: Of course! I spent my day writing and strangely it was fun!

This brief message only showed a gram of the excitement in me.

Eugene: That's great! I need to tell you

something...

The three little dots at the end were never a good sign.

Sol: Go ahead...

Eugene: I just learned that Bruno is indeed Kylo and that we are related.

Sol: Okay, wow!

Even if I gave him the benefit of the doubt, Bruno still was a suspect. That "related" part I did not expect. The statement left me in shock

Sol: Are you sure?

Only to assure myself did I ask.

Eugene: I am sure. I also found the other reason Kylo killed Lokki.

Sol: We should meet and discuss this in person.

I sent out—not believing in the privacy we were guaranteed by telephone companies.

Eugene: Not at the Cherry.

Sol: Sure. What about we go to a café in the street next door, the one with the ballroom?

Eugene: I'm on my way.

Sol: Copied and pasted.

Witty had become my middle name.

My writing session had been cut short, and

I practically ran out happy to see Eugene, to drink an excellent coffee and learn more about our past situation, as it could help me with the book.

Another message had come.

Eugene: I found a coffee shop, it's called Blue Cup, and it's right next to the ballroom.

Sol: Can't believe we missed it the first time.

Eugene: Believe.

My wit rubbed off on him and I liked it.

All the way to our meeting place, I did my happy walk, which was basically an adult skipping around town looking like she was in a good mood—which she was.

Once at the cute rustic café, I spotted my boyfriend with two cups in front of him. Yes, my boyfriend.

"Hello, boyfriend," I told him, removing my coat and placing it on the back of the chair. It was bliss how it rolled off my tongue. I'm an adult and I've never had a boyfriend. Sue me.

"Hi, girlfriend," he replied, copying the grin plastered on my face.

"Long time no see."

"Too long," he said with a teasing kind of pout.

The urge to hit that arm placed on the table was... Let's say immense. I was an adult with self-control. I poked him instead.

"I went ahead and ordered you something new."

I switched my range of view to the drinks on the table when I took notice that both were in paper cups, meaning they both were hot. I let some sort of small awkward chuckle out—it described the emotions I felt at that precise moment.

"I know you don't drink hot stuff, but open the lid."

Opening the lid, I melted like the ice of my morning coffee. There was a heart drawn on the foam, the other surprise was the colour of this mysterious drink. It was blue.

"You can't really do latte art on cold coffee. The barista recommended me this item. It's a blue butterfly tea latte."

"Hold on, you mean a butterfly was harmed for my happiness?"

"I would never buy it if they made it with butterflies. They used a flower called butterfly pea."

"Oh, I see, well thank you."

"That's not all. Apparently, a blue butterfly represents the soul and means hope, change, and new beginnings."

"That's all so meaningful and sweet, but does it taste good?" I asked him, by accident, sounding like I did not care at all for his touching act, but I did. It's just that my only drink of the day was awful.

"I haven't tried it yet. I was waiting for you."

"That's so sweet!" Now, I wouldn't care even if it tasted like dirt.

"Cheers," he said, leaning my cup towards mine.

With a sniff, I was charmed. It had a candle scent to it and a baby blue appearance. With a sip came the unknown. A burst of flavours familiar yet unique. We both matched eyes and boy were they large. We were equally shocked at how good it tasted and were left to be speechless. Although it was only a flower, some milk, and most definitely some sugar, it was jaw-dropping.

"This has to be the best thing I've ever tasted... After coffee."

"It is a close second."

"They say you learn and experience something new with your soulmate every day. I didn't know it would be up to that extent."

Chapter

23

Eugene's point of view

Soulmate. Coming out of her, it sounded swell. There was no way I'd take my eyes off of her. She drank the tea latte with joy, every sip a new expression. Raised eyebrows the first, risen lip corners the second and cheekbones reaching the eyes for the third.

"How have I never heard of this delight?" she said, going for more. Wiping the foam off her lips, she spoke again. "Didn't you have something to tell me? Like the other reason Kylo murdered Lokki." she whispered that last part getting closer to me. Sol did well, as the place was busy for a small coffee shop.

Leaning my head nearer, I whispered directly in her ears: "Kylo was jealous since Lokki had many girls dying to date him, but he chose Cosi. And he thinks Lokki did it on purpose to piss him off." That part really didn't need to be whispered, as it wasn't too sensitive. Still, the intimacy was thrilling.

"That doesn't make sense," she said, pulling back, sadness clouding her features.

"It doesn't."

"How can he destroy such a love story? How could a few words from him turn it all so meaningless?"

"It can't. His words don't have that kind of power. It was and will always be a great story. Lokki and Cosi's love was genuine. I'm sure you can feel it in your guts just like I do."

Sol nodded, her voice turning airy. "I do feel it."

"Now the bad news."

"There was bad news?"

"It can't be helped in this story."

"Shoot it then."

"I'd prefer not to."

"Shoot" or "stab" were sensitive words now. But obviously, I was joking. And it was always fun to see her startled face.

"I'm sorry, I meant: give me the news." A sudden laugh blew my cover and I, for the first time today, got my well deserved hit on the arm. I don't think Sol is the violent type. Those hits aren't even qualified to be called hits. She barely puts her force in them, making them playful strikes.

"I'm sorry too. Alright, the bad news is that I provoked him earlier."

"How exactly did you provoke him?"

"I told him I loved you."

"Aw. I mean, why? I mean, aw, that's so sweet. I love you too, but I now understand that provoked him."

She had multiple faces. In one breath she went from touched to angry to touched again to understanding.

"It came out by accident and thank you for loving me back."

Her habits were way too contagious and my immunity system grew weaker in her presence. When did I ever become such a romanticist?

"Was he very mad?"

"There's something else."

"Will the sun even set today?"

"After this last thing, it will."

"I need a sip from the happy drink before I can hear anything else."

"I think Bruno was born with Kylo's memories, or maybe they came to him throughout his childhood because he honestly feels the anger Kylo did. He speaks with the spitefulness I would expect Kylo to have."

That explains why he hated me since day one, when I hadn't even made contact with Sol. He recognized me.

"Well, that's alarming. He had a reason to kill you all along. Not a good one, but still one."

"Maybe not me. Remember the butterfly effect? The switched coffee preference?"

"Yes, but that was a theory. What reason would he have to kill me?"

"If he can't have you, nobody can kind of reason?"

"I'm getting chills." Her face paled, and she held my hand. "He's a psychopath!" That, she whispered, grimacing on every syllable.

I place another hand on hers, stroking it gently. "I will not let him touch a hair on you. Trust me and stand by me." We may go on this camping trip sooner than I thought.

"How fast can you pack your bags?"

"We're leaving town?"

"Only for the camping trip."

"In the middle of the biggest crisis of our lives?" she said, lowering her head, her chin reaching her neck.

"I'll be at peace knowing you'll be by my side 24/7. Bruno won't know where we are."

"We can't stay there indefinitely. We'll come back and I doubt Bruno would, by miracle, move away and or forget about his lifelong grudge."

She had a point.

"I was too hasty."

"You had good intentions and I thank you for that." Her hand toppled over mine.

Our hands looked like a hamburger with double cheese, double meat and double everything.

I gave a trembling sigh.

"I'll think of something we can do. Put your trust in me," I told her, but she shook her head, confusing me.

"*We'll* think of something. Don't take the whole burden for shoulders. I want a piece too." How amazing was it that no matter how dark or terrifying the situation was, we both managed to sprinkle humour in? It may be a coping mechanism making it all look sad or bring suspicion to our childhood. I saw it as something positive.

"It's not like we can go to the police," she continued. "If only there was a paranormal or supernatural police in town. I wouldn't be surprised if there was with all the weird rumours flying around."

"Rumours?" It intrigued me. I had arrived here not too long ago and was either stuck at home or at the Cherry. I didn't sightsee or hear anything about Mardi Town.

"They say vampires lived here, and they even had a private club which may still exist and if vampires are immortal, they probably left and created a new identity somewhere else because they are forever young. Who knows, maybe one of them could come back here someday after it's been long enough that the people of his olden days passed away." She rambled on about vampires and only a couple of days ago, I would've said that there was no way. Now, I don't even need to spell out my answer. Anything could be possible.

"You know, maybe Cosi and Lokki had a vampire in their circle or maybe…" A far-fetched idea came to mind. It's even silly that I mentioned it. "What if Bruno was a vampire?"

Sol started a gasp, stopping halfway. "If he was alive in the 30s, he wouldn't be so out in the open today where people would remember him."

"Yeah, it was dumb of me. I don't know what to think anymore."

"Think of our solution."

"What solution?" I heard a wicked voice say. It was Bruno, who was a couple of steps behind Sol. I stood up and pulled Sol's chair to my side. I held her hand tight and gave the dirtiest look I could give to Bruno. He might have beaten me to it. Death was written all over his face.

"Whoa, I'm not a monster. What are you doing, buddy? Oh, were you making space for me? Why thank you."

"You're not welcome here, Bruno," Sol had said, reminding me of her message to Lokki.

In front of her were Kylo and his past acts. In the cemetery, she had mentioned a certain revenge. It made me nervous to see her so inflamed. I wanted to spare her from the atrocities and not let her jump into the fire.

"Why not, sweetie?"

I had already cracked his neck, in my mind, for having called her *sweetie*. Bruno—without a care—pulled a chair from a nearby table and sat down, facing us.

"We never said you could sit," I snapped.

"This is a public place, buddy."

He entered the place with a cocky smile that now looked permanent. He was ready to mess things up.

"What are you even doing at another café?" Sol started. "Did you follow us like Kylo did in the past?"

"You walked into your own grave," he said, not looking at a specific person. "I have something to tell you, Sol. I thought I could at least try, since I missed the chance to say it in the past."

"Shoot." This time, she did not hold back the sensitive words. In fact, it may have been a threat.

I felt useless when they both talked. I was only the person holding her hand while she fought.

"Then and now, his love wasn't sincere. Lokki back then only thought you were interesting because you didn't approach him, while many did. A lifetime might have passed, but he's the same. He has the same mentality. He will never love you and he'll never treat you right."

"And you can?" replied Sol. The toying had begun.

"Yes! There's no one who loves you as much as I do. I thought of you every single day in my past life and in the current." Bruno sounded desperate.

She had opened a door in his heart he longed to be opened. It's as if he had rehearsed his speech every day.

"Why did you let me die?" Sol had said, her voice deepening.

"I didn't know you would do such a thing."

It was fascinating to listen to this conversation. Sol had taken the role of Cosi and Bruno believed it.

"Did you ever regret killing Lokki?" she asked him, a stern look on her.

"I never did." Game over, buddy.

"You've just admitted that you don't love me." Bruno's face dropped. "If you really loved me, you'd want to keep me alive even if I was away from you. Not regretting means you'll do it again, knowing I'd die from it."

"I'd do it again, but I would not let you end yourself. I'd be by your side, comforting you."

"You do know you sound ridiculous, right?" I had to add my two cents.

"There will be no next time, Bruno."

"I tried, Sol. I tried to give you a chance."

"You're crazy. Why would you be the one to give me a chance?"

"I tried to have a happy ending with no brutality but..."

"But?"

Sol's point of view

My heart dropped. My spine tingled. My insides spun. I wanted to run away. If possible, teleport Eugene and I out of here. Bruno was insane. His threats weren't so empty. I saw it in his eyes. Everything was so clear there. I could see his intention with the naked eye. His last resource was the one we feared. My only thought was to protect Eugene, and I suppose he thought the same of me. I wanted to turn away from the horrendous stare contest I had with Bruno. I so deeply wanted to look into

Eugene's warm eyes and feel the comfort of his chest. I shouldn't take my eyes off of Bruno, I thought. In a swift second, it all could end. In the past, Cosi couldn't see, nor did she know Kylo was with them. It could have been avoided if they both knew. We knew we sat facing him. We talked with him and had a chance.

Bruno had embedded fear in his dialog. Even a blink seemed like stepping on a mine. No matter how much Eugene squeezed my hand, I didn't look. I bit my lip with teeth that felt sharper than usual. I may also have pierced through the skin of my own hand with fingernails. My nerves manifested into odd self-destructive habits. Finally, I snapped. In the blink of an eye, I opened the lid of my warm drink and threw it on Bruno's face. I didn't have the time to feel all the attention that was brought on me since I ran out, dragging Eugene by the hand.

"Sol!" Eugene called out.

"This is serious," I told him, clenching my jaw.

I couldn't bear to look back. Fear had invaded me. If anything could slow me down, I'll avoid it.

Protect Eugene at all costs. These words were engraved in my brain. It was all coming down, and I didn't want us to lose anything. The climax of the story had approached, and I wondered if I'd be able to write the ending of the story or I'd have to leave it to my successor. We were being chased; I knew it. I recognized Eugene's panting and another one farther away. We hadn't run long and were already cornered.

"Stay behind me, Sol," he told me, pushing me to a white wall in the narrow alley between the Blue cup and the ballroom.

"Well, well, I told you that you walked into your own grave. Don't you recognize this place?"

The universe wanted to kill us. What did the universe have against us? In one of our previous lives, did we team up to start a galactic war and destroyed planets and stars? Lokki was killed behind the ballroom. No matter how many things changed, the planets aligned again. Our feet, in the end, entered the lion's den.

"You killed Lokki behind the ballroom. We're across it," Eugene remarked.

"If that detail bothers you, we can head out there. It's no problem." His mockery made me want to punch him, and I've never punched anyone before. Not wanting to be sheltered by Eugene and letting him be the target, I escaped. I stood at his side, horrifying him.

"Don't, Sol," he said, keeping a gentle tone. Even in a dire situation, he hadn't raised his voice at me. This was the man I would put my life on the line for.

"We'll do it together and this is Bruno," I said, pointing to the man who showed us bare hands. "It's not Kylo. You think those hands who only made coffee will take us down?"

He let out a scoff. "Who said I came empty-handed?"

Bruno took out from the pocket of his jeans a kitchen knife with a guard on. I had a hunch he came prepared, but I didn't know they had kitchen knives in coffee shops. It's maybe for the sandwiches. By instinct, we stepped back. Unfortunately for us, we hit a cold wall.

"Bruno, we are not in the 30s. You can't kill someone for the sole reason a girl chose him over you."

"You can't kill a girl for the sole reason

she'll never love you and you don't want to see her loving someone else."

Eugene and I both laid different reasons relayed in a similar manner. It didn't seem to work. Bruno took a few steps ahead. The urge to scream for help suffocated me, but my voice didn't come out. The terror paralyzed my limbs along with my throat.

"I'm crazy, crazy for you, Sol." Hearing his voice pronounce my name was torture. I had only wanted to pronounce him dead.

"What do we do, Eugene?" I whispered to him, every part of me curling.

"Nothing will happen to you," he whispered back, worrying me.

He said you not us. Eugene was planning to sacrifice himself for me because there was no other way out.

"I love you," he said.

"No!"

Lokki's last line had been the same. Bruno removed the guard and walked towards us. With tightly shut eyes and a sense of urgency, I rushed to the front, shielding Eugene with my body. Not seeing anything, I felt my body being whacked away with great force. Of course, I thought it was Bruno. Opening my eyes, I had received the biggest shock of my life. Eugene was on his knees, a knife planted in his stomach. Wincing in pain, his eyes crinkled. My knees had dropped as well.

"I didn't really mean to do it," I heard Bruno say.

With trembling hands and troubled eyes, he dropped the knife and ran away. Now my hands were trembling, tears came out rolling and I couldn't figure out what to do. Blood flowed out of his wound onto the floor. Eugene looked at me, almost choking, and reached his hands towards me.

"Stay with me, Eugene," I told him, panting. "We're in 2022. We can call an ambulance." With hands that relentlessly shook, I rummaged through my bag for the phone. Getting a hold of it, I immediately pressed the emergency call button.

"I- need help! Someone- has been stabbed! Please come quickly. We are in an alley behind the Blue cup café on Aveberry street."

Eugene had managed to take a hold of my hands. He looked at me with eyes that hadn't lost their shine.

"It's... gonna be... alright," he said with great difficulty.

With all the tears, my vision turned completely blurry. I yearned to hold him in my arms but that would hurt him even more, seeing there was a knife in him. The only thing I could do was touch his hands. I brought them to my lips and kissed them a hundred times.

"You bet it's gonna be alright. They'll bring you to a hospital and they'll fix you. I am not letting you lie down and die here. No way!" I broke down. "You'll live." He had given me half a smile.

From afar I could hear the sirens, they sounded like bells angels would ring.

"Hold on for me, hold on. Don't close your eyes." I pleaded, desperately holding on.

The pool of blood had reached my own knees. He paled. Drops of sweat fell from his forehead and neck. There was nothing I could do but wait. I wished I was the one to have been stabbed. I wished to have been the one receiving the excruciating pain. I wished he'd never had to experience this. To say that my heart hurts would undermine his pain.

The blood mixed with sweat and tears diluted and, like a river, it went long. Hard boots stepped on the red liquid. Looking up, I saw men and women in uniform rushing to

Eugene, hands pushing a stretcher.

"Please, be careful," I told them, my voice breaking.

I knew they were professionals who knew better than me how to treat a critically injured person. At the time, nothing had made sense, and the light was farther than the darkness that invaded our space. I watched them hold Eugene from every limb as they placed him on the bed. He now laid on the flat area. With the remaining force I had, I took his hand and followed the wheels rolling to the ambulance.

"The person who stabbed him ran away! His name is Bruno, and he works at the Cherry street coffee shop!" I screamed to the people who remained behind. I doubt Eugene could hear anything during his battle, but I bet he'd be proud I didn't let angst completely take over my rationality.

In the ambulance, they asked me a couple of questions and wrapped a blanket around me. Eugene had received minimal first aid with the knife still in him. It was a terrifying sight. A mask on his face helped him breathe a little better, but the pain, I'm sure, was still unbearable. This could not be the end. We still had so much to do together. So much to learn about each other. Those few days were not even qualified to be called a complete beginning. We were so young, with years ahead of us. We had to walk side by side, with a cane in one hand and a hand in the other. He told me we deserved our happy ending. I think so too.

***

At the hospital, serious faces were followed by serious faces. There came a time I couldn't follow him anymore since he entered the surgery room. The possibility of it being the last time I saw him alive made me want to rip my heart out. I sat on the floor, all alone, letting the tears silently roll down. I was falling. I begged to the universe who ruined us so many times to bring him back to me. The bond we have is tight. We are soulmates! I believe it with my all. His loss would be a weight I could not carry. I understood Cosi more than ever. I was Cosi.

Amid my despair, a man in a white gown tapped on my shoulder.

"You came with Eugene, right?"

"Yes!" I jumped and stood so fast that I got

lightheaded and almost fell unconscious. The doctor held me up by grabbing an arm.

"I came to tell you he'll be okay. He was lucky the person who stabbed him wasn't very able with knives. He missed the vital spot and took a random jab."

"Oh, thank you." The relief had manifested itself in me with deep exhales, making me even dizzier. The doctor had brought me to a seat in the waiting room, but I refused.

"I need to see him. Is he awake?"

"He'll be in a couple of minutes. I can bring you to his room. You can sit there and breath slowly. It's you who we should put under oxygen." That slight humour I liked so much lifted my spirits a bit.

Walking in the room, Eugene laid on the hospital bed with closed eyes. He looked at peace, finally having a knife removed from his body and a bandage placed in its stead.

Bringing the chair as close as I could to the bed, I sat. I held the hand I'd been holding so tightly on the way here and tenderly stroked his beautiful face with my other hand.

"It's over. We'll have our happy ending," I said. "Thanks to Bruno's stupidity." Tears of rejoice and remaining sadness filled my eyes, once again.

"Stupidity?" a groggy voice said.

"You're awake!"

"Of course I am. You're the stupid one now. I promised you it'll be alright." He opened his honeyed eyes and gave me that smile. The one where his lips curved more upwards than sideways. The warm cup of milk Cosi talked about. I couldn't take it anymore. I leaned towards him and aimed for the lips. We had only kissed three times, and I initiated two of them.

"There's something else I promised you," he said, holding my hand dearly.

"Was there something else?"

"I told you we'd go camping at the beach. At first, it was an excuse to keep you away from danger. Now I feel I'll enjoy it more. Staring at the waves, doing a campfire."

"No, no. We're not going anywhere when you're this hurt."

"Maybe we'll wait a couple of days."

I let go and pushed myself back.

"Days? You mean weeks."

"How can I wait this long?"

"You'll wait. In the meantime, we could plan

this trip."

"I already planned it."

"When did you find the time for that?"

"I've always thought about it. It's a dream of mine."

"Dream stealer," I told him, sticking my tongue out. I was the one who had a dream with him at the beach. He copied it.

Eugene laughed at my childish behavior and soon regretted it. Holding his stomach, he shut his eyes tight and pressed his lips together—frowning. Worried, I rushed to him.

"Don't you laugh anymore."

"How can I when the mere sight of you makes my lips curve?" Even in pain, he spoke such sweet words.

I wanted nothing more but to cry. Holding it in, I wrapped my arms around his neck. Lower than that was off limits.

Dear Eugene, I hope my every moment is spent with you.

Epilogue

Three weeks later

"Finally, we're here," Sol told Eugene. They both sat on canvas chairs planted on the cool sand. Eugene, wearing his classic black hoodie, stretched to her side and planted a peck on her cheek, right on top of the faint freckles.

"I told you we'd come. I always keep my promises."

"I'll keep mine as well."

"I don't doubt it."

They sat at ease, knowing the worst had passed. In their range of view, waves smoothly crashed, one after another.

"I can't believe it all ended."

"Believe already," he said, restless.

"We'll never come across Bruno again, not

in this lifetime, I guess." Speaking out his name gave Sol chills, but she went on. "He was caught, yes, too bad it was only for attempted murder. He did murder Lokki. On other thoughts, physically, it wasn't him."

"The spiritual laws will take care of him in their own ways," Eugene added.

"You mean with karma?"

"Yes, maybe we've been freed from a large amount of negative karma and Bruno still had his to encounter."

"I hope so," she said, the end of her feet reacting.

"Let's forget about him and have a good time." Eugene leaned forward, leaving only his bottom on the chair. "I have a surprise for you."

"Wasn't this trip the surprise?"

"Not the end of it." Without giving further explanation, he walked to the back.

Sol kept her eyes on the water, which appeared to near the legs of their chair only to pull back halfway. Following the trail of miniature waves had made her drowsy and heavy-eyed. By then, Eugene had already made his way back to her with a black guitar case in his hands. Sol's eyes soon lightened and her entire body perked up to look at him.

"You know how to play the guitar?"

"Not really," he grimaced, taking a seat. "I bought it a while ago at a thrift store and learned a very small amount of cords because I found this." Opening the case, he took out a glorious leather jacket. The ripped edges only added to its charm. Leather jackets were known to become more attractive with age.

"Is this *the* jacket?" Sol asked, her hands on her wide open mouth.

She waited for a nod of his part to confirm. It couldn't have been any other jacket but Lokki's. The curling of his lips and she had her answer.

"I know it's the jacket since I found these inside." From a hidden pocket, he brought out crumpled papers that looked to have been burned and revived by how golden they were. Hand written words were carved in black ink. Sol reached out her hands to grab them. Before she could, Eugene took them away.

"I'm not letting you read them. You'll only

listen."

"What could that mean?" she responded, sarcasm in the air she exhaled.

"This, I believe it belongs to you." To her surprise, Eugene cosily wrapped Sol in the leather jacket.

"Cosi was right, it does smell nice. I didn't expect it to due to his old age. It smells like fabric softener." Sol fell deep into her paradise until it all clicked. "Did you have it dry-cleaned?"

"I wouldn't let you wear something dirty."

A smile formed on her face. "Where did you find the jacket, anyway?"

"Luck was on my side."

"Care to explain in words I can understand?"

"Alright," he started, "a couple of days after they released me from the hospital, I went to visit Lokki and Cosi's graves. It was a spontaneous visit. When I was in front of Lokki's grave, an old man approached me. He said he almost got a heart attack. He told me I was a photocopy of Lokki. As a kid, he resided in the same neighbourhood as him. They often played together, and he recalled how Lokki brought him pieces of chocolate every so often. In the end, hc told me he's found and kept the leather jacket as a way to remember him. Seeing me, he thought it was fate and handed it to me. He said something along the lines of: This jacket seems to belong to you." He let out a sigh. "Long story short, I guess."

"I'd remember a person who gave me chocolate." Sol said, visualizing the tale she'd just heard.

"I better buy a stock of chocolate."

"Now, Eugene, you have to think a little. Why would I forget the person who's constantly on my mind?"

They laughed at their silly words, holding each other's hands.

"Let me show you what I prepared," Eugene continued. He took out the pearl white guitar from its case. "Lokki left the lyrics in his pocket. I'm sure they're the songs he wanted to sing at the Cherry for Cosi. I'll do it in his stead. It won't be as good as him."

"It doesn't have to," she said in a heartbeat. "Though you look alike, you are two different people. It's a new life with a new destiny. The body might not only be a vessel, it seems to be much more." Sol smiled at him, warmth in her voice.

Eugene turned a shade brighter and scoffed to hide it. He positioned his guitar. "If I'd been stabbed on the other side, I might not have been able to play."

"How's your wound, by the way? Any better?"

"Much better," he assured.

"Be honest!" her cheeks puffed, annoyed with the mask Eugene wore.

"It's still a little sore."

"Thank you." She longed for his honesty. "Now you can start."

A stroke to the guitar, a mischievous look to Eugene, and the first note was laid. A few more strokes, and began a sweet melody. His lips parted, letting the sweet words escape.

"I thought it was all a dream,
You looked at me with those lovely eyes,
You made me breathless,
My heart stopped,

And now I tell you I love you,

I swayed on my own for long,
Long enough to know,
That I couldn't bear it any longer,
You came in with cadmium green heels,
Swept me off my feet,
I am obsessed with the idea of you,

You make me love sick,
You bring my mind places its never been to,
I'll tell you again and again,
Even a million times,
I'm deeply in love with you,
Please accept my words and live to be a hundred with me."

Sol, speechless at what she'd heard, covered her mouth. If honey had a voice, it would be Eugene's. Every word was sung delicately with emotion. He had perfectly revived the jazzy flow of the 30s while conveying his and Lokki's honest feelings.

Embarrassed by his first performance with

a very exclusive audience, he hid the guitar behind him.

"Is there anything you can't do, Eugene?" Sol truly questioned it. "And why hide the guitar? Wasn't there another song?"

"Another day, I've done enough." He squealed, his face buried in his hands.

"I'll let you off easy this time, if you do me this one favour."

"Shoot."

"When you have the time, record yourself singing this song."

"Why would I do that? I'm a photographer, not a singer."

"I'm not asking you to send it to a talent agency. I want to keep it in my phone and listen to it every day, once in the morning and once at night."

"You do me a favour, too. I want to take a picture of you with the moon."

Eugene stared at the night sky where a full moon magnificently shined.

"Doesn't it look like the moonbow you wanted to photograph?" Sol remarked while observing the colourful faded circles around the moon.

"It resembles it, but it isn't quite a

moonbow." He took out his camera and clicked on the right buttons. "Show me that pretty face," he said, hoping she'd turn around and face him. "It's beautiful," he said, clicking on the shutter.

245

"I hope my every moment is spent with you," Sol said while Eugene thought it in his mind.

The end

Acknowledgments

Thank you to my mother, who believes in me and constantly shows interest in my work.

Thank you to my father, who lets me ramble on about my books on our weekly coffee shop outing.

Thank you to my dear friends for having sent me supportive messages. They were such a motivation when the work was tough. You know who you are.

At last, thank you, my reader, for giving my book a chance. I hope you enjoyed it.

Coming soon

Six more books are to come for the Mardi Town series. There is no need to read all the books in order since the only connecting point is the location. A few fun cameos will occasionally be shown, but they will not bring spoilers with them.

Come again to the lovely old-fashion Mardi Town and meet plenty of different protagonists, they have so many stories to tell you. With an open mind and an open heart, join me, will you?

www.ingramcontent.com/pod-product-compliance
Lightning Source LLC
Chambersburg PA
CBHW072014210726
48294CB00011B/684